GOLDEN EMPIRE

In the remote mountains of Southern California, the Rio Kid unearthed a nightmare conspiracy. A powerful Master of Evil was forcing helpless Chinese workers into barbarous slave camps. Torture and death awaited any man who challenged his maniacal dreams.

Undaunted, the Rio Kid stole his way to the hidden camp. Captured, wounded and outnumbered, he faced the showdown of his life. But dead or alive, he vowed to squash the rising Empire of doom!

Dudley Dean was the name Dudley Dean McGaughey used from the beginning for his series of exemplary Western novels written for Fawcett Gold Medal in the 1950s. McGaughey was born in Rialto, California, and began writing fiction for Street & Smith's *Wild West Weekly* in the early 1930s under the name **Dean Owen**. These early stories, and many more longer pulp novels written for Masked Rider Western and Texas Rangers after the Second World War, were aimed at a youthful readership. The 1950s marked McGaughey's Golden Age and virtually all that he wrote as Dudley Dean, Dean Owen, or Lincoln Drew during this decade repays a reader with rich dividends in tense storytelling and historical realism. This new direction can be seen in short novels he wrote early in the decade such as "Gun the Man Down" in *5 Western Novels* (August 1952) and "Hang the Man High!" in *Big-Book Western* (March 1954). They are notable for their maturity and presage the dramatic change in tone and characterization that occur in the first of the Dudley Dean novels, *Ambush At Rincon* (1953). *The Man From Riondo* (1954), if anything, was even better, with considerable scope in terms of locations, variety of characters, and unusual events. *Gun In The Valley* (1957) by Dudley Dean, *Chainlink* (1957) by Owen Evens, and *Rifle Ranch* (1958) by Lincoln Drew are quite probably his finest work among the fine novels from this decade. These stories are notable in particular for the complexity of their social themes and psychological relationships, but are narrated in a simple, straightforward style with such deftly orchestrated plots that their subtlety and depth may become apparent only upon reflection.

GOLDEN EMPIRE

Dean Owen

GUNSMOKE

This hardback edition 2006
by BBC Audiobooks Ltd
by arrangement with
Golden West Literary Agency

ISBN 1 4056 8079 2

British Library Cataloguing in Publication Data available.

Printed and bound in Great Britain by
Antony Rowe Ltd., Chippenham, Wiltshire

CHAPTER I

The Sentence

□ There was a grim silence along "officer's row" at Fort Tejon, high in the mountains above the great valley of the San Joaquin. The officers, some of them fresh from the "Point," others seasoned veterans, would turn now and then to stare at the C.O.'s headquarters where the trial was being held.

One of the younger officers resplendent in a new uniform strolled up to the other commissioned men. "I might as well have Sergeant Starke look over the scaffold and see if it's in working order," he said.

First Lieutenant John Curtin, who had fought with Fremont and carried an old arrow scar across his neck, whirled on the younger officer.

"Don't jump at conclusions, Michaels," he snapped. "It's up to the court to decide the penalty, not you!"

Second Lieutenant Michaels flushed under his brother officer's direct gaze. "Regulations say there is only one penalty for deliberate murder," he reminded Curtin. "Death by hanging."

"The devil with regulations," Curtin retorted, his face whitening. "Barling is a fellow officer."

6

Michaels drew himself erect, his gray eyes boring into Curtin's tense features. "Barling is a murderer," he said. "He shot a man in the back for a pouch of gold coins. Just because his victim was Chinese is no cause for leniency."

Lieutenant Michaels' voice carried across the drill ground so that enlisted men, lounging before the barracks, began to edge closer. They sensed trouble was brewing and wanted to be in on it.

The hot sun of desert and mountains had burned young Michaels' face so that the skin was peeling in several places, which did not add to his West Point dignity. His hands were soft. His uniform showed good tailoring and gave him a well-cut figure, but it was plain that he believed he could show these veteran officers what it took to be a good officer. He lived by regulations in a country where regulations were forgotten more times than they were remembered when the going was rough.

Curtin's fists were balled and he took a threatening step toward Michaels, who was the taller of the pair.

"I made no reference to the murdered man's color," he said, answering Michaels' accusation. "A dead man is a dead man, whether he be white or yellow. But I don't think Barling is guilty."

Young Michaels, impressed with his own dignity and apparently intent on showing these backwoods officers a thing or two, smiled contemptuously.

"Now who's jumping at conclusions," Michaels said. "If the facts are as I've heard, then there will be but one verdict."

A sunburned lieutenant spoke up. He was Linderman, recently transferred from Fort Yuma. "You're making a spectacle before the men," he warned sharply and pointed to the troops who were drawing closer.

With an arrogant swagger Lieutenant Michaels turned his back on Linderman and spoke over his shoulder.

"You forget I was one of the witnesses against Barling. I never liked him and I hope his neck is stretched."

Lieutenant Curtin swore and would have followed Michaels, but Linderman put a restraining hand on his arm.

"He doesn't like it because Barling was commissioned from the ranks," Linderman said. "That is unthinkable to an Academy man."

Lieutenant Michaels halted before the barracks and singled out a rough, bearded sergeant.

"Sergeant Starke," he called.

Starke came to rigid attention, his right hand flashing up in a smart salute. It was plain that Starke was following regulations, saluting the uniform, not the man. There was dislike that was hard to conceal in his dark eyes.

"Check the scaffold," Michaels ordered, pointing toward the skeleton-like structure at the foot of an oak-covered hill beyond the drill ground. "Oil the trap spring and get a new rope from the quartermaster. I want it rigged for a hanging. Report back when you've finished."

The two men saluted. Starke called out half a dozen troopers and led them stiffly across the parade ground. The other troopers drifted back into the barracks, obviously wishing to avoid the ire of this green lieutenant.

Back with the officers now, Michaels said, "It isn't often that a Fort has the privilege of hanging a First Lieutenant in the United States Army."

Curtin glared up at the swaggering officer. "You're a blood-thirsty devil," he snapped. "I'm wondering how you'd stack up against a score of renegade Indians."

Michaels gave his brother officer that superior smile. "I know how to deal with renegades, white or red," he answered.

Tension grew between the two men and again Linderman had to intervene. "You're liable to get the C.O. down on you, Michaels," he said, "ordering a scaffold inspection without hearing the verdict."

"I'll take my chances."

At that moment the door of Headquarters opened and half a dozen officers filed out. A tall, fair-haired lieutenant, surrounded by troopers, rifles at the ready, was marched across the drill ground to the guardhouse.

Captain Sam Bordolus, hands clasped behind his back, walked slowly toward the group of waiting officers. They exchanged salutes.

"What's the verdict, Captain?" Linderman asked.

"Life. It was his record that spared him from the noose. Life at the stockade on Alcatraz Island."

Lieutenant Michaels stiffened. "But that was cold, deliberate murder, sir," he complained.

"So the facts might indicate," Bordolus said with a scowl.

"You mean to say there is some doubt of his guilt?" Michaels demanded.

"I've known Lieutenant Barling for a long time," the captain fairly shouted. "He's a good officer. I don't like to think he is guilty."

"That's preposterous," Michaels said in an awed tone.

For a moment the captain bristled, then relaxed. "Lieutenant, those are my personal opinions, not the opinion of the trial board," he said slowly.

"But life for murder—"

"It would be more humane to take Lieutenant Barling out and shoot him," Bordolus said bitterly. "I'm sure he would rather have it that way. Life imprisonment in the Army means one thing, life imprisonment. No hope of freedom, ever."

With that, Captain Bordolus strode toward his quarters. The other officers drifted away, one by one, leaving Michaels standing alone, fists clenched at his sides.

Then he walked quickly to the C.O.'s headquarters. He was gone only a few moments. When he returned he found Lieutenant Curtin just crossing the drill ground.

"I've requested special duty," Michaels said.

"What duty?" Curtin asked suspiciously.

"I'm in charge of the detail that will escort Barling to Alcatraz," Michaels replied with a tight grin. "We'll see what kind of stuff an officer commissioned from the ranks is made of."

CHAPTER II

Rey Manilla

☐ Brightly, the westering sun threw a last stab of golden light over the great flats of the San Joaquin, while to the east the gray-blue barriers of the Sierras were already masked in the purple shadows of evening. Two horsemen moved up the steep winding Army road, pausing to look back at the valley from which they had come.

"We've put a lot of miles behind us, Celestino," the tall rider on the dun said with a smile.

Celestino Mireles' dark eyes lighted appreciatively as he stared at the scene of beauty.

"These hills seem peaceful, General," the Mexican answered. "We have the quiet journey to Los Angeles."

Captain Bob Pryor neck-reined the dun horse. Celestino had called Pryor "General" since the distant day when he had saved the Mexican's life in a border raid.

Celestino Mireles urged his pinto up the zig-zag trail behind Captain Bob Pryor, known throughout the West since the Civil War as the Rio Kid. The sound of a bugle blowing "Retreat" came to them on the evening breeze.

"Only a few miles to Fort Tejon," the Rio Kid said. "Then we'll pick up a bait of grub."

The road leveled off, winding through a canyon that was flanked by round-topped hills. Here and there oak trees dotted the slopes and a few head of cattle grazed off the road.

"Lieutenant Barling is stationed at the fort," the Rio Kid said over his shoulder. "I haven't seen him in three years, since he was at Yuma."

His blue eyes lighted with expectancy as he looked forward to the reunion with his old friend.

"You can talk over the old times, eh?" Celestino said with a grin, his white teeth flashing in the gloom.

To the Rio Kid it did not seem more than a few months since he had been an officer in the war. Then he had been one of the most courageous young officers in the Union Army. As Captain Robert Pryor he had executed daring missions throughout the bloody years, winning commendations from Generals Grant, Custer and Sheridan. A Texan, Pryor, like many another young frontiersman from the Lone Star State, had to weigh his loyalty. It was either state or country. He chose to be loyal to his country and was proud that he had a small part in helping to preserve the Union.

Now that the war was over, he carried on his dangerous life from border to border and from the Missouri on the east to the Pacific on the

West. His restless nature would not allow him to settle down in one place and give up his adventurous existence.

He was a handsome man in his blue Army shirt, the dark whipcord breeches tucked into polished boots and the campaign hat slanted recklessly on his head, only partially hiding the close-cropped chestnut hair.

He was the ideal height and weight for a cavalryman. Crossed cartridge belts slung from his slender waist, held twin Colts. Another brace of guns were carried beneath his shirt. Captain Bob Pryor was a true fighting man, strong neck, rugged shoulders and narrow waist.

There was no fear in him, for he had adopted a fatalistic view of life. A natural leader, many famous men of the West had come to rely on his judgment and deadly guns.

With Celestino Mireles always at his side, the Rio Kid welcomed any assignment of danger.

The Mexican had the pure blood of the hidalgos in his veins. Hawk-faced with snapping black eyes and raven hair, Celestino was a colorful figure with his high-peaked sombrero, tight-fitting velvet pants, and stitched jacket. Beside the gun at his belt, he carried a *cuchillo*, razor sharp.

These two had been inseparable since the day, years before, when raiders had attacked the rancho belonging to Celestino's family. After killing his parents, the renegades were about to finish off Celestino, but at that moment the Rio Kid had arrived on the scene and driven them back.

Saber, the Rio Kid's war horse, was an unprepossessing mount with wicked teeth and a temper to match. No one else but the Kid could handle him. He had been trained to face enemy fire without stampeding, and for speed and endurance he had no equal. Saber had two characteristics, a mirled eye which would roll when he was angry, and a black stripe which ran down his back. This stripe would quiver whenever he sensed danger and Bob Pryor had come to rely on this as a signal that trouble awaited him.

To the Rio Kid it was like coming home to enter the main gate at Fort Tejon and see the smart troopers, the trim buildings and the spotless parade gound. A chill wind was blowing up as they dismounted before the C.O.'s headquarters. The Rio Kid announced that he wanted to pay his respects to Major White, in command.

In a moment the orderly returned wearing a broad smile. The Rio Kid followed him into the building and found Major White behind a long table, studying a stack of carefully penned reports. His snapping steel-gray eyes came to rest on the Rio Kid and he arose to extend a square hand across the table.

"Captain Pryor," he boomed in a voice that was loud for so small a man. "Sheridan has spoken highly of you. I'm glad to have the privilege of knowing you."

"I had heard that you were commanding here," the Kid said with a friendly smile.

Then for the first time he noticed the dark man who stood against a far wall. The man wore a fancy leather hunting jacket and soft cowhide boots. His almost yellowish features were inscrutable. He kept watching the Rio Kid out of yellow eyes.

"Captain Pryor," the Major said, "I'd like you to meet Rey Manilla."

The two men shook hands. When the Kid looked into Manilla's eyes he felt a thread of warning sing along his nerves. There was something unwholesome about this man with the Oriental features. Pryor sensed that Manilla was the kind who would enjoy putting a knife in a man's back and then twisting the blade.

"It is a pleasure to meet you, Captain Pryor," Manilla purred. His speech was accented with the almost imperceptible intonation which belongs to the Chinese. Manilla seemed well-armed. There was the bulge of a big gun under his coat, and the Rio Kid saw the pearl butt of a derringer protruding from his vest pocket.

Living constantly with danger, Pryor had acquired the habit of sizing up a man at first glance. Sometimes it spelled the difference between life and death. Now a sixth sense told him that Manilla was not a man to be trusted.

"You'll sit at my table, Pryor," the major said. "It's almost time for mess call."

When the Rio Kid explained about his trail mate, Celestino, the major readily included him in the invitation. Major White told his orderly to have Celestino turn the horses into the stable where they would be cared for.

Manilla put a black, flat-topped hat on his greasy dark hair, explaining to the major that he must be on his way to Los Angeles.

Manilla was halfway to the door when the Rio Kid asked the major a question.

"I've been looking forward to seeing Lieutenant Barling," he said. "Is he here?"

Major White's jaw fell. Manilla whipped around to stare, sudden interest sparking in his yellow eyes. A scowl centered between Pryor's blue eyes as he wondered at the sudden silence in the room.

"Barling's stationed here, isn't he, Major?" the Rio Kid asked in surprise.

Major White spread his blunt fingers in a helpless gesture. "Lieutenant Barling is under arrest," he said, avoiding the Rio Kid's sharp gaze to look out the window where a detail of blue-clad soldiers marched toward the barracks.

"What's the charge?" the Rio Kid asked. Barling had always been a fine type of officer and Pryor could not understand why he would be arrested.

"Barling has been convicted of murder," Major White said in a low voice. "He shot a

Chinese merchant in the back. A man by the name of Chang Wah."

"You got proof of that?" the Rio Kid demanded, forgetting at the moment that the major as C.O. probably headed the trial board.

"I'm sorry to say there was proof," White answered.

"Barling was one of the finest young officers I knew," Pryor snapped. "It's sure hard to believe that he'd be guilty of shootin' a man in the back."

"Here is the report," the major said, and tapped the stack of papers on his desk. "These are being forwarded to Washington."

So astounded was the Rio Kid at this news that he did not notice that Rey Manilla had come to stand beside the table.

"You do not think Barling would be capable of murder," Manilla said coldly.

"No, I don't," Pryor answered, wondering at the man's interest in the case.

Major White, noticing the tension that was building up between the two men, stepped between them.

"Manilla was the chief witness against Barling," he explained.

At this news the Rio Kid's dislike of Manilla crystallized into hatred, for he sensed the man knew more about Barling's guilt than he was telling.

"I don't know the facts in the case, of course,"

Pryor admitted. "But I'm willin' to bet every cent I ever hope to have that Barling ain't guilty."

"You are the same as calling me a liar, sir!" Manilla cried.

Red anger flashed across the man's slant eyes and he lifted the tail of his coat to reach for the butt of his gun. It was a practiced draw, smooth and instinctive.

The Kid's balled fist was whipping out and when his knuckles thudded against Manilla's jaw, there was all the force of his powerful shoulder behind the blow.

Manilla had tried to duck but he took the smash and fell against the table, then tipped forward to spread his lean dark length on the scrubbed boards.

"I'm sorry you did that, Pryor," Major White snapped. Then as he saw that Manilla was out cold, a barely perceptible twinkle appeared in his eyes. "I've had the urge to do it myself for a long time."

The orderly appeared, drawn by the sounds of the fight. He left, then reappeared with a glass of water. Manilla sat up, shook his head as if to clear it, then got to his feet. He clutched one end of the table to steady himself, glaring at the Rio Kid who stood there rubbing his knuckles.

"You're impetuous, Pryor," he said coldly. "Some day I may take the time to rectify your mistake in assaulting me."

"There was no need to lose your temper, Manilla," Major White rapped out. "I haven't liked this case from the start. That is why Barling received a life sentence instead of the death penalty."

Manilla allowed a cold smile to touch his thin lips. "A thousand pardons, Major," he said suavely, trying to hide the thread of anger in his voice.

Ignoring the Rio Kid completely, Rey Manilla bowed to the major then left the room. Outside, he was joined by a blocky man who wore his black hair long and was attired in greasy buckskins.

"Who's the gun-hand?" the Rio Kid asked as he watched the pair through the window.

"Mike Jarel," Major White answered. "Another witness."

Halfway across the parade ground Manilla stopped and conversed for a moment with a young lieutenant. The two men shook hands and Manilla climbed into the saddle of a gray gelding while Jarel mounted another horse. They followed a lumbering freight wagon out the gate. Two men were on the seat of the freighter and there was a saddle horse tied to the tailgate.

"Manilla seems friendly with one of your officers," the Rio Kid observed.

"That was Lieutenant Michaels." White

growled. "As you know I have no choice but to accept any officer who's assigned to this post."

The Rio Kid gave him a sharp glance but the major did not clarify his statement.

"Would it be asking too much if I visited Barling?" the Kid asked, when the major had finished gathering up the stack of papers and had turned them over to his orderly.

"Ordinarily I would not grant such a request," the major said, after a moment's hesitation. "But perhaps you—" He bit off the rest of the sentence, as if suddenly remembering that he was the commanding officer of this fort.

"Thank you, Major," the Rio Kid said after the officer had scribbled out a pass. "I got a hunch to hear Barling's side of this story."

CHAPTER III

The Prisoner

☐ Mess call was sounding outside now but Pryor had no thought of food in his mind. He wanted to see Barling and learn first hand from the young officer his version of the affair that had resulted in a life sentence.

Outside, the Rio Kid took the pass Major White had given him and held a quick consultation with Celestino. The young Mexican's face grew grave when he learned the news that the Kid's old friend had been found guilty of murder.

"But General, you do not believe this Senor Barling is guilty!" he said quickly.

"Of course I don't," the Rio Kid replied, as he stared down the road where he had last seen Rey Manilla. "I sure don't like the looks of the complainin' witness."

After telling Celestino to meet him at the mess hall, Pryor crossed the drill ground to the guard house. Here he showed his pass to the guard on the door and was allowed to enter the big log building.

The guard house at Fort Tejon was one large

room, with heavy barred windows and a grille that cut the room in half. In the forepart the two guards were stationed.

The Kid was not allowed in the cage so he had to stand by the bars while the guard shouted Barling's name. There were only a dozen or so prisoners in the place.

When the Rio Kid saw the tall, fair-haired young officer step forward, he hardly recognized him. There were deep lines in Barling's face and bitterness in his eyes. He crossed the cage with dragging steps but, even though the stigma of murder rode his shoulders, he held his head high.

The lanterns had not been lighted yet, so it was nearly dark in the room. It wasn't until he was at the bars that the lieutenant let out a whoop of joy at sight of the tall, square-shouldered frontiersman before him.

"Captain Pryor!" he shouted so loudly that the guards and the other prisoners swung around. The two men clasped hands through the bars.

"It's been a long time, Barling," the Rio Kid said soberly. "I sure didn't figure you'd ever be in a tight like this."

At the reference to his sentence the officer's face clouded and he gripped the bars so hard that his knuckles whitened against the metal.

"You've heard the whole rotten mess then," he said in a voice heavy with defeat.

"But I haven't heard your story," the Rio Kid reminded him.

And these encouraging words, probably the first he had heard since his arrest, brought a light of hope to Barling's eyes.

He was tall and fair, with a well-muscled body. He had clear eyes and a good jaw. It was his explosive temper that had caused him minor trouble in the past. He was commissioned from the ranks during an Indian uprising at Fort Bowie. When his commanding officers were killed, Barling took over and saved the platoon from annihilation. He was a true soldier, but embittered now at Army red tape and his prison sentence.

"You're the same old Captain Pryor," Barling said. "You never believe ill of a friend."

"Tell me what happened," Pryor said softly, so that the other prisoners would not overhear. "I'm going to get you out of this."

"Captain, you know that an Army court-martial is as final as Judgment Day," he said with a shake of his head.

"Don't give up hope," the Rio Kid said quickly, grasping the officer's arm through the bars. "You didn't get the noose and that's something. Now we have more time to work."

Barling's jaw hardened. "The whole thing is so crazy that I can't believe it myself," he explained. "I'd been out on patrol getting a few head of cattle that had been run off by the Indi-

28

ans. I sent my men on into the fort and I loitered along the way. I heard gunfire and immediately rode in the direction of the shots."

"What'd you find?" the Rio Kid asked, when Barling hesitated.

His voice was grim when he answered.

"I found an old Chinese, dead, shot through the back. Nearby was his mule but nothing more. He looked like any of the coolies you see up north. I searched him for identification but found no papers."

"Where did Manilla come into this?" Pryor asked.

Barling's lips tightened. "I was stooping over Chang Wah when Manilla and his two men jumped me. They covered me and accused me of killing the Chinese. I was arguing with them when Lieutenant Michaels rode up. He and I had had some words the day before. Michaels listened to Manilla's story, then took great delight in herding me back to the fort. I was put under arrest. You know the other details."

"It seems like Michaels sure came in handy," the Rio Kid remarked after a moment of speculation. He was remembering how Manilla and Lieutenant Michaels had shaken hands there on the parade ground. "I'm beginning to wonder what connection there is between Michaels and this hombre who calls himself Rey Manilla."

Barling shrugged. "You know the Army. There was nothing I could prove in my defense.

29

When they searched my locker, they found a sack of Chinese coins. As Chang Wah had similar coins in a money belt, it was assumed that I had cached part of the loot on the post before having a chance of disposing of it."

"That's flimsy evidence," the Rio Kid snapped.

"But evidence enough," Barling said bitterly. "Somebody planted those coins. I had no defense. They even said that, because I was to be married next month, I had stolen the money so as to have a suitable start for married life."

"Anyone who really knew you would never think a thing like that," the Rio Kid growled.

"It was Michaels' theory."

"Sure seems like he's got a lot to do with this," Pryor answered.

"There's more to the trouble than meets the eye," Barling went on. "You see I knew Chang Wah. I lived in San Francisco as a boy. My father and Chang Wah were very friendly. Chang's son Chang Lee and I were practically raised together."

"Mebbeso, but why would he be comin' up here?" the Kid asked in surprise.

"I have a feeling it was to see me," Barling answered.

"Well, the Chinese have been havin' some bad times in California lately," the Kid said. "Mebbe it had somethin' to do with that."

"I'm sure of it," Barling said. "I told the court

that I knew Chang and that he was a wealthy merchant. Manilla said that was why I had killed him."

The Rio Kid rubbed a hand across his square jaw and stared down at the board floor, still damp from its last scrubbing.

"You're goin' ahead and gittin' married on schedule," he said.

Barling bared his teeth in a hopeless smile. "Let's face facts, Captain," he said grimly. "I've been sentenced to life at Alcatraz Island. I haven't any chance of clearing myself." He struggled with the next words. "I was to marry Beth Price, a school teacher in Los Angeles. If you get down that way will you do me a favor?"

"Sure, I will, Barling."

"Tell her I was accidentally killed in a hunting accident," the prisoner said bitterly.

"That's not bein' very fair to her," the Kid said.

"Fair," Barling almost shouted. Then after a quick glance at the other prisoners, he dropped his voice. "I'll never get to Alcatraz. I'm going to escape or—I'll never go there to rot on that island."

"Don't lose your head," the Rio Kid warned, remembering the man's explosive temper.

"Anything is better than Alcatraz," Barling snapped.

"Just don't give up hope," Pryor reminded him.

"Hope?" Barling said with a tight laugh. "I leave at sunup for Alcatraz. And Lieutenant Michaels has charge of the detail. I just heard the news from some of my," he paused a moment, "ex-brother officers."

The news that Michaels was going to be in charge of Barling's trip to the military stockade in San Francisco Bay was disturbing.

"Give me Beth Price's address," the Kid said, "and tell me all you can about Lee, Chang Wah's son."

Barling scribbled out his financee's address, then shook his head when he started to tell about Lee.

"The last I heard he had gone to Los Angeles to open up a shop," he explained. "That was months ago. No telling what has happened since then."

The Rio Kid knew what Barling meant. These were uncertain times for the Chinese. Politicians were seeking office, saying that the hard times were due to cheap coolie labor. There was talk of shipping all of the Orientals back to China.

"I'll try to locate Lee," Pryor said as he shook hands with Barling. "And I'll see Beth Price."

"Give Beth my message," Barling pleaded. "I'd rather have her think me dead. She'll be free to marry someone else. If she knows I'm spending my life in prison, she may live in hope that some day I'll be free. And you know the Army better than that."

Even though the Rio Kid realized the whole thing looked hopeless, he gave Barling a reassuring grin and left the guard house.

In the officer's mess Major White introduced the other men to the Rio Kid. Pryor liked Lieutenants Curtin and Linderman and Captain Bordolus. He found Lieutenant John Michaels to be a smooth-cheeked overbearing soldier, a synthetic officer. It was apparent the other officers knew the Kid was a friend of Barling's, for the conversation was carefully steered away from the subject of the trial and the sentence.

Celestino glanced up from his plate to give Pryor a reassuring grin.

After supper, the Rio Kid strolled across the drill ground with Major White.

"Major," Bob Pryor began, not quite knowing how to express the thoughts that were in his mind, "I understand Lieutenant Michaels is goin' to be in charge of the detail takin' Barling to Alcatraz. Do you reckon—"

"I know what you're thinking, Pryor," Major White said quickly. "Michaels has no use for Barling. I know if I sent Curtin or Linderman or one of the other officers they might be inclined to let Barling escape. I cannot have that happen. After all, this is the United States Army and there is no room for personal feelings."

They had reached Headquarters. Beyond the

star-filled sky rose darkly above the rounded peaks.

"I don't trust Michaels," the Rio Kid said grimly.

"He'll be accountable to me," Major White snapped. "If Barling is harmed in any way, I'll break Michaels if it's the last thing I ever do."

"Thank you, sir," the Rio Kid said and left the major.

That night when Pryor and Celestino had bedded down in the storeroom, they had a consulation. Each agreed that Barling's plight was tied in some way with the Chinese question. Orientals were disappearing. No one seemed to know what had happened to them. Their property was being taken over and sold on the open market. So far, the general public did not know these things, and those responsible were evidently intent on keeping it from them as long as possible.

"I think we'll catch up to Rey Manilla," the Rio Kid said as he lay in his blankets. "Mebbe he'll give us some information, if we persuade him right."

CHAPTER IV

Ambush!

☐ Early the next morning a stiff wind was blowing dark clouds across the rounded peaks and there was the smell of rain in the air. A summer storm was blowing up. Saber stamped the ground and nickered when the Kid threw on a saddle and tightened the cinch. The dun was glad to be hitting the trail again and it seemed as if his instinct told him his master was going on another mission that would end in the rattle of gunfire and the smell of powdersmoke.

With Celestino at his side, the Rio Kid rode out through the main gate and along the road that led to Los Angeles. The road followed a high plateau. Even though they were at an elevation of four thousand feet the peaks were more like hills than mountains and there were no pines, except on the higher slopes to the west. A stiff wind caught at their hatbrims as Pryor set them off at a gallop.

"I figure we kin catch up to Manilla before noon," the Rio Kid said. "He won't make much time with that freighter."

Celestino showed his white teeth in a grin and

touched the butt of his fancy gun as if anticipating the trouble to come.

A half hour later they passed a stage depot. The corral held a relay team but there was no one around but the stock boy. He was a furtive-eyed youth who seemed more than casually interested in their arrival. At the Rio Kid's question he admitted that Manilla, with his wagon, had spent the night a quarter of a mile up the road.

"We better keep our eyes open from here on in," the Rio Kid mused as he and Celestino hit saddle leather again. "Manilla's the kind of a gent who would like to line a gun on your back."

"Maybe like he do the *Chino*, Chang Wah," Celestino put in.

The Rio Kid nodded, his keen blue eyes taking in the sparse wooded slopes, crowned by the stormy sky. Instead of following the road now, he gave the signal to cut across the low ridge which would save them several miles. Saber's hoofs dug into the firm footing of the hillside and soon they had reached the crest. A small valley lay below, but now they were in the clouds and they had only intermittent glimpses of the flat lands which lay beyond.

It was only long habit of caution which caused the Rio Kid to look back the way they had come. Higher up on the plateau he could see the stage station only a tiny dot in the distance. But that was not what caught his eye. It was the column of black smoke which funneled skyward beside the building. Celestino noticed it, too, and the dark skin over his cheek bones tightened as he pointed to the black puffs which broke off, then rose again.

"Injun smoke signals," the Mexican said excitedly.

"It's that hombre at the station," Pryor said, sun wrinkles at the corners of his eyes deepening as he studied the smoke. "He's probably usin' a creosote fire and a blanket."

They both caught the smell of wood smoke in the strong wind which blew against their cheeks.

"Maybe Manilla paid the kid to signal if we come by lookin' for him," the Kid said wheeling Saber and sending him down the slant. "Keep your gun unlimbered," he warned over his shoulder.

Suddenly the heavens abruptly seemed to open, for a torrent of water spilled down from the sky. Lightning flashed and thunder rolled like a thousand cannon, shaking the ground and causing Celestino's pinto to rear and snort in fright.

They were on a rocky shelf and the going was slippery in the rain. The skittish pinto lost his balance. Celestino, superb horseman that he was, could do nothing but leave the saddle.

The Rio Kid saw him go, rolling up in a tight ball to take up the shock. He whirled Saber, made a grab for the pinto's reins, but at that moment a bullet whistled past his ear and a rifle blasted off to his left.

It was rough going in the mist that had suddenly descended on the valley. But as the fog cut aside he could see a heavy freighter pulled off the road in an oak grove, the team still in harness.

"Keep down, Celestino!" he yelled as he saw a shadowy figure ahead near the wagon's tail gate.

Celestino had regained his feet and was now scrambling over the slippery shale, gun in hand. The Rio Kid let the panicky pinto go plunging off into the stand of wet green oaks. Only the brief space of half a dozen clock ticks had passed since that bullet had *whooshed* through the air close to his head.

The Rio Kid knew if he retreated he would leave Celestino unprotected. Therefore he drew his brace of six-guns, let Saber have his head and guided the horse with his knees. He headed straight for those boulders where three guns were opening up on him from behind a cluster of boulders near the wagon.

Guns blazing, the Rio Kid put Saber at a zig-zag run. A man's sombreroed head appeared above the rocks. The skulker was evidently confident he could pick off this reckless horseman.

The Rio Kid fired both guns instinctively. The stranger threw up his hands to fall back out of sight. Bullets from two other guns were singing their deadly song. It was an eerie sight here in the mountains with rain slicing down from a black sky, and fog making a ghost world out of this battleground. Now Celestino's gun was added to the chorus of blasting weapons.

But Celestino was in plain sight. Now the Rio Kid pressed Saber with his knees and the gallant, trumpeting horse whirled in a tight circle. The Rio Kid galloped back the way he had come, to cover his partner. It was treacherous going on the slippery shale and any second he expected Saber's iron shoes to slide, but the horse kept his balance.

When the Kid reached Celestino's side, he noticed the firing had ceased. There was the diminishing thud of hoofbeats but the Rio Kid knew pursuit would be foolhardy in the dense fog.

"They have gone, no?" Celestino said, as he walked up, smoking gun in hand.

The young Mexican seemed unruffled at his narrow escape from death. There was an unspoken bond between these two. More times than once they had saved each other's lives, and the Rio Kid again had simply covered the Mexican at risk of his own neck.

Together they moved toward the boulders. The storm had tapered off to a light rain by this time. They found the dead man sprawled on his back, a hole in his forehead.

"What do you think has happened?" Celestino asked in a low voice, peering into the rain-shrouded oak grove where they could see the freight wagon.

"There ain't no tellin' what their game is," the Rio Kid answered with a shrug. "You take a look over there while I search this hombre."

Without a word, Celestino made his way through the wet brush.

The dead man was smooth-shaven, wearing a flannel shirt, black pants and scuffed boots.

His mouth was agape, his eyes staring at the gloomy sky.

The Rio Kid went through his pockets with deft fingers. He found some coins, tobacco in an oilskin pouch and a small leather bound book. Sitting on his heels, his broad back to a rock, Pryor opened the book.

What he saw written on those pages brought a whistle of surprise to his lips. There was a list of Oriental names, and opposite the names were items of property. Some of the items mentioned were a laundry, a gold claim, art store in San Francisco and gambling house in Stockton.

A grim smile crossed the Rio Kid's lips. For the first time he felt he had some tangible evidence that he could work on. Now he was making progress.

Celestino returned, his fancy belled trousers wet from the brush.

"There is nobody about," the Mexican reported. "I see tracks where two riders go south. But I find this."

He tossed a piece of folded paper at the Rio Kid's feet.

"That's a Chinese lottery ticket," Pryor said triumphantly. "Unless I'm off the track, I'll bet Chinese were hauled in that wagon."

"There ees nothing else in the wagon, General," Celestino answered.

"I reckon we've got Manilla worried," the Kid said grimly. "He fixed it with the stock boy at the stage station to signal if we was on his trail. That give him time to set the ambush. Now I reckon Manilla's got important business in Los Angeles. Otherwise he wouldn't have pulled out."

They buried the dead skulker there beside the road. Then the Rio Kid mounted Saber and began a hunt for Celestino's pinto. He found it grazing a quarter of a mile up the hill. They unhitched the freight team and turned the horses loose. There was no time to take them to a corral and it would be cruel to leave them tied up.

Now they rode hard and fast, catching snatches of sleep under the stars or in some shady place by day. It was apparent to the Rio Kid that Manilla had left with one of his men even before the ambush was sprung. Otherwise they would have been able to overtake him by this time.

One scorching day the Rio Kid and Celestino rode out of the tules along a dry river bottom to see the Los Angeles plaza, the church and the sleepy little pueblo, which was feeling its growing pains. To the south and west they could see

evidence of the town's expansion since their last
visit here.

Skirting the plaza, they stabled their horses in
the Queen corral. There the Kid took special
care of Saber, working him over with curry
comb, then giving him a can of oats.

The stableman, a fat, tobacco chewing man,
who had the perpetual smell of horse sweat
about him, sidled up.

"You gents are just in time to ride in the
Fourth of July parade," he said. "It forms at the
plaza."

"Sorry, we got other business," the Rio Kid
told him with a grin, and saw the disappointment
on the fat man's face.

They learned that the parade was supposed to
start at noon, but the fat stableman still could not
induce them to participate.

After breakfast at a small cafe beside the Pico
House, the two trailmates went to the plaza, a
block up the street. Small boys were shooting
firecrackers which they had purchased in one of
the Chinatown alleys. There was an old Army
field piece which was to be fired at the start of
the parade. It was being primed now.

Los Angeles was in a festive mood this Fourth
of July. Banners were hung from building to
building across the street, while below a water
wagon traveled the length of Fort Street settling
the dust. The crowd began to gather early,
women dressed in their best finery, men in their

43

Sunday suits. There were small boys, scrubbed and waiting for the cannon's roar which would signal the start of the parade. A couple of mounted deputy sheriffs warned the spectators against throwing firecrackers into the street so as not to frighten the horses and perhaps cause a runaway.

Celestino grinned with pleasure as he watched the excitement.

"Thees Independence Day is fun, eh?" he said.

"It's the day we remind ourselves of a couple of things," the Rio Kid answered gravely. "That freedom has been won, and that it sure can be taken away mighty quick."

He was thinking of Rey Manilla and others of his kind who had tried to pursue their policy of greed. And he knew that man could cause a bloody scourge of guns and death to sweep the peaceful hills of Southern California.

As these thoughts spun through his mind the cannon roared. The crowd applauded and a band began to play. The Rio Kid and Celestino crowded forward to watch the parade come swinging down the street.

And in the first carriage was a man the Rio Kid had long admired, the man who had first raised the stars and stripes over Los Angeles— General John C. Fremont.

He wore a flat-brimmed hat, but now he waved it at the crowd as a mighty roar went up at his recognition. Fremont sat erect in the carriage with the bearing of a born soldier. His beard, neatly trimmed, gave him a simple dignity. Even his critics had to admit that he was a man of great courage, a man of foresight who had pioneered much of the West when it was more of a wilderness than it was this day.

The acclamation of the crowd swelled as the carriage proceeded down the street. Citizens lining the building tops began tossing confetti and tissue streamers, so that by the time the shining black vehicle had gone a block it was crisscrossed with the bright-colored strips of paper.

"I'm glad to see that folks here still remember Fremont," Pryor told Celestino. "Sometimes it's easy to forget a great man like him."

Now came the volunteer fire department, the engine shiny, the crew's helmets glistening in the noonday sun. Then there were two carriages filled with aging veterans of the War of 1812. These men got a wild reception from the crowd which had come here from the smaller towns and the ranchos that surrounded Los Angeles.

There were grandees riding their palominos, dressed in all their finery. These men, some of the last great rancheros, were a hold-over from a more peaceful era of California. They brought color and a touch of romance to the parade.

At last the procession was over and the crowd surged into the street. There was the snap-snap of Chinese firecrackers. Women screamed and lifted their skirts as the sizzling red cylinders exploded at their feet. A town marshal marched a drunken cowboy off to jail. An old bearded plainsman pulled out his gun and thumbed half a dozen shots at the cloudless sky.

As the Rio Kid and Celestino continued their search for Rey Manilla, a horseman, mounted on a splendid midnight black, came cantering up through the crowd.

Pryor was watching the rider, noticing the way he sat the saddle. This man was a born horseman. He had seen the stranger in the parade, riding directly behind Fremont's carriage.

Now the rider swung close to the boardwalk.

"Pryor, Captain Pryor!" he called.

The Rio Kid and Celestino halted, watching the man make a quick dismount to lead his horse by the reins.

And as the Rio Kid got a closer look at this man he recognized him as Alexander Godey, one of Fremont's famous scouts.

CHAPTER V

The Plot

☐ Alexander Godey and the Rio Kid shook hands and Pryor liked the firm handclasp of this fighting man.

"I've sure heard plenty about you, Godey," the Kid said. He introduced Celestino. "This man was Fremont's best scout on all his expeditions," he explained to the Mexican.

Godey and Celestino shook hands, then the famous scout sobered. "Fremont spotted you in the crowd, Pryor," he said quickly, lowering his voice. "He pointed you out to me and I came hightailin' back here soon as the parade was over."

The Rio Kid felt his nerves tense, for it wasn't like a man of Godey's reputation to be concerned unless it was serious.

"I didn't reckon Fremont knew me," Pryor answered.

"There ain't a frontiersman livin' who ain't heard about the Rio Kid," Godey answered quickly.

Then Godey looked around to see if he was being overheard. "If you kin spare the time,

Fremont would sure like to palaver with you," he said turning back to the Kid.

"I ain't never too busy to talk to a man like Fremont," Pryor answered.

"Good," the scout said. "Fremont's stayin' at the Pico House. Room three-twelve. Can you be there at three?"

The Rio Kid nodded. The men shook hands again, then Godey mounted and rode back the way he had come.

"What do you theenk he wants, General?" Celestino asked.

"I dunno, but I got a hunch it's somethin' mighty important," Pryor said. "I thought Fremont looked kind of worried. He didn't seem to be enjoyin' himself and I wondered why."

"We find out soon, no?" Celestino said, as they walked up the crowded street.

"I wish it was three o'clock right now," the Rio Kid said grimly.

The Pico House was the most ornate hotel in Los Angeles, and it was crowded when the Rio Kid elbowed his way through the lobby and climbed the plush-carpeted stairs to the third floor. They had spent the time until the meeting, trying to find some lead on Chang Lee, son of Chang Wah, the old Chinese merchant Lieutenant Don Barling had been accused of murdering.

Celestino was in the Chinese quarter now, trying to carry on the search. He was to meet the Kid in the stable later.

In a moment the Rio Kid was knocking at the door of three-twelve. Almost the instant his knuckles touched wood, the portal was opened and General John C. Fremont was clasping the Rio Kid's hand, pulling him into the room.

"Captain Pryor!" he boomed, a note of excitement in his voice. "This is a lucky day for me."

He closed the door and the Kid took a chair he had indicated. Alexander Godey, lounging on one end of the fancy brass bed, lifted a hand in greeting.

"I don't see how you recognized me, sir," the Rio Kid asked, a puzzled frown on his forehead.

A smile stole over the general's lips. "I saw you at Fort Yuma several years ago," he said. "I have a good memory for faces."

Godey shifted his weight on the bed and the springs groaned under his weight. "Better get to the point, General," he put in. "We've got to catch the five o'clock stage. And there's that reception the mayor's fixin' on givin' for you."

"You're right, Alex," Fremont said and began pacing the carpet to trace out the pattern with his booted feet.

"Captain Pryor, I know your reputation," he began. "You have done splendid work, ridding the West of some of its worst sore spots."

"I reckon you and Godey have done a heap more," the Kid said modestly.

"Your work has been harder," Fremont said quickly. "Undercover work is always more dangerous. You haven't received the recognition you unquestionably deserve."

"The satisfaction of doin' a good job is all the recognition I want," the Rio Kid said.

"I never knew a good fightin' man who didn't like to belittle his own accomplishments," Fremont said with a grin.

Then his bearded face grew serious and he began pacing the floor again. Fremont had the boundless energy, the clear sharp eyes of the pioneer. This man had dared to blaze trails that others had feared. And the Rio Kid, sitting in this hotel room, overlooking the Los Angeles plaza, knew that he was indeed flattered to have the general regard his ability so highly.

Fremont wore a neat black suit, a starched white shirt. The gold watch chain across his vest was the only spot of color in his attire.

Even when he paced the floor, he did it vigorously, as if he could not wait to step out of these confining walls and once again go trailing over the mountains with his old companions of those early history-making expeditions.

And the Rio Kid thought how much the nation owed this man, who had come to the Pacific Coast to plant the Stars and Stripes, beating the other foreign powers who were eying the territory with greedy eyes. If it had not been for his accomplishment, California might now be flying a very different flag.

"Captain Pryor, I hate to leave my beloved

California, knowing that disaster may undo all the good that has been done."

The Rio Kid tensed at the general's words. "You talk as if you weren't coming back to California," he said, impressed by the somber tone in the famous officer's voice.

"The general has just been named Territorial Governor of Arizona," Godey said from the bed.

The Rio Kid congratulated Fremont, but the general waved it aside.

"There is a pattern of bloodshed that is going to grow until there will be a blot against the fair name of California that can never be erased," Fremont said gravely.

"That's serious talk, General," the Rio Kid said.

"It is serious," Fremont snapped. "It's the Chinese question."

Pryor could not help but sit up more alertly in his chair. Fremont nodded. "I see you're interested," he said.

"I am interested," the Rio Kid replied. "One of my friends faces a lifetime in the military stockade on Alcatraz Island and it's tied, in some way, with the Chinese trouble here in California."

"Let's compare notes," the general said, his eyes lighting with anticipation.

Quickly the Rio Kid sketched Barling's conviction of murdering the elderly Chinaman,

Chang Wah. He told of Rey Manilla and the attempted ambush on the road to Los Angeles.

When he had finished, the general looked at Godey, who had been listening intently to the Rio Kid's recital of the tragic events.

"Well, Alex, I told you Captain Pryor works fast," Fremont said. "Now he knows nearly as much as we do."

"What about this Rey Manilla?" the Kid asked. "Who is he?"

"He's an Oriental, a breed of many races," Fremont said. "He's wanted by the British and French for piracy. Nobody knows how he got into this country, or how he stays. It's his knowledge of Chinese which has enabled him to work his scheme against the coolies and merchants."

"Looks like he's the man we've got to get," the Kid admitted.

The general went on to outline all he knew of the dark plot against the Chinese. The thousands of Orientals who had been brought to California to help build the Central Pacific railroad were without work in most cases, now that the railroad had been completed. Under these circumstances they were being persecuted, and the current wave of unemployment in California was being laid to the Chinese.

"Now that I'm a Territorial Governor, I can't afford to mix in California politics," Fremont added. "Alex is going to Arizona with me,

Pryor, on another matter. But if you could uncover this diabolical plot and bring the culprits to justice, you would be doing your country a great service."

Quickly the Rio Kid's bronzed face lighted with a grin. "I've already started on it, General," he said. "Me and Celestino will sure enjoy hangin' Rey Manilla's hide to the fence."

"But Manilla's isn't the only one," Fremont put in. "I suspect he's taking orders from some powerful political figure. He's the man we've got to get."

Pryor got to his feet, the tension mounting within him so that he could not sit still.

"Anything else you can tell me, General?" he asked.

"John Searles, a good friend of mine, runs a borax mine on the desert at Searles' Marsh," Fremont said slowly. "It's not far from Indian Wells. He was in town last night and told me he's seen a stream of Chinese going into the eastern side of the Sierras."

"And they never come out," Godey put in grimly.

"This is beginnin' to make sense," the Rio Kid said, and told them of the list of Chinese names and items of property he had found on the dead skulker near Fort Tejon.

"That looks like you're on the right track, Pryor," the general said, excitement edging his voice.

Alexander Godey came up with a suggestion.

"You've got an invitation to Coronel's *baile* tonight, General," he said. "You're leavin' town. How about givin' it to Pryor. He might be able to pick up some information. All the big wigs'll be there."

"Good idea," Fremont cried, and crossed the room to a chest of drawers. He opened the top drawer and came back with a square of cardboard in a white envelope.

"Antonio Coronel is a Spanish don and a true Californian," he said. "Alex has a good idea. So why don't you and your friend visit the ball?"

He scribbled something on the back of the invitation, then gave it to Pryor.

"Remember this must be done under cover," Fremont warned. "If the Army has to do the job it will bring California into the limelight. I don't want that to happen. If we work fast, the whole plan can be smashed before the majority of people even suspect what is going on."

"Nobody'll know about it," the Rio Kid assured him.

Now the famous general placed a hand on Pryor's shoulder. "This is dangerous work," he said in parting. "I'd give a lot to be able to stay and see this thing through."

"So would I," Alexander Godey put in.

"Don't worry, General," the Rio Kid said with a measure of confidence in his voice. "I'll be lookin' forward to the day I can write and tell you that Manilla and his boss won't be a threat any more."

"Good soldier," Fremont exclaimed. "I knew I could count on you. And I'll be waiting for that message."

CHAPTER VI

The Challenge!

☐ During this period in California, the famous adobe *casa* of Antonio Coronel was the social center of Los Angeles and, as the Rio Kid and Celestino approached in the darkness, they could hear the strum of guitars and the laughter and chatter of the guests. Carriages pulled up before the entrance and bejeweled ladies and their escorts alighted to be met by Coronel himself.

Pryor and Celestino entered a walled garden and crossed the patio. Here in the moonlight they could see many couples strolling in the shadows. Inside there was the soft glow of candlelight.

Antonio Coronel's patrician features relaxed when the Kid showed him the invitation. His graying head bobbed over the message Fremont had written. He smiled and extended his hand.

"A friend of General Fremont's is a friend of mine," he said in perfect English. "I am sorry he could not come."

Then he shook hands with Celestino and conversed with him for a moment in their native language.

There was an orchestra at one end of the low ceilinged room and now a fiddler was busy tuning his instrument. Tossing their hats on the table reserved for headgear, the Rio Kid and Celestino mingled with the crowd. It seemed that everyone of importance was here at the *baile*. Light from the candelabrum caught the blue fire of diamonds.

More than one feminine eye was turned upon Captain Pryor as he moved about the great room. With his close-cropped chestnut hair, his bronzed face and strong features, he was a striking figure. With the colorful Mexican at his side, they made an unusual pair at this Independence ball here in the *casa* of Antonio Coronel.

It was after the music had started that the Rio Kid heard the host greeting a young lady.

"The Senorita Price is always welcome," Coronel said with a smile. "It is too bad that I am old, otherwise I would return to school and be in your class. You would be my favorite teacher."

The Rio Kid's blue eyes had narrowed at the old don's words. Now he felt Celestino's fingers clutching his arm.

"Perhaps it ees the betrothed of Lieutenant Barling," the Mexican whispered.

"Might be," Pryor answered tensely, and leaving Celestino with his back to the adobe wall, crossed the room. He was just in time to see a lovely dark-haired girl giving her wrap to an Indian servant.

"Are you Miss Beth Price?" Pryor asked over her shoulder.

She had her back to him and now she turned quickly, the hem of her skirt whipping above her slender ankles.

"Yes, of course," she replied with a questioning lift of her dark brows. For a moment the haunting shadows that had been apparent in her eyes vanished. She tilted her head to one side to study this grim-faced man.

"I'm a friend of Don Barling," the Kid said, drawing her into the shadows of the patio.

He saw the faint flush that stained her cheeks and the smile that quirked the corners of her mouth. She began to talk excitedly of Barling, wondering how he was, if he were coming soon to Los Angeles.

"This is goin' to be hard, Miss, but I want you to know it ain't as bad as it sounds," he said seriously.

The girl's lips tightened. She wore a gay, jeweled comb to relieve the dead-black of her shinning hair that was piled upon her head Spanish style.

Tall and supple, the full roundness of her was not entirely hidden by the folds of the rustling satin dress she had worn to the ball. Now that they were alone, Pryor felt her warm fingers against his hand as she begged for news of her fiance.

And as he talked, telling of Barling's trial, and

subsequent sentence, he wondered at his own rashness in projecting a note of optimism. After all, he was up against intrigue so sinister that even General Fremont, famous liberator of California, was concerned.

The color had drained from Beth Price's cheeks and now she turned quickly to hide the tears which had suddenly come to her dark eyes.

"He didn't want you to know," the Rio Kid said, patting the slender shoulder in a gesture of sympathy. "I figure we can get him free. General Fremont knows about it, and as soon as we git to the bottom and line up the facts, he'll put in a good word for Don on my say-so."

She faced him again. "I'm glad that Don has a friend like you," she said in a low voice. "You've given me courage. On top of—of everything else that's happened, I don't know whether I could carry on."

"Somethin' else troublin' you, Miss?" he asked.

"It's my father," she said, evidently having full confidence in this new friend. "He's disappeared."

"California's a big state. Maybe he's just—"

"I'm afraid he's in trouble," she said. If you ever get up into the Sierras, look for Amos Price. He took a freighting job with a man named Rey Manilla."

The Kid's nerves tensed at this information. He didn't tell her of Manilla's connection with Barling, for she had enough to worry about.

"I'm leaving tomorrow by stage for Indian Wells," Beth Price said. "That was the last place Dad wrote from."

"Don't leave here," the Rio Kid warned, taking her by the arms to shake her gently. "Indian Wells ain't no place for a girl. I'm goin' there on business. I'll look up on your dad."

"And talk to this man, Rey Manilla."

"I'd like to talk to him with a gun in my hand," the Rio Kid snapped.

"What is it you're sayin' about Rey Manilla?" a voice cut in at his elbow.

Pryor whirled, his nose wrinkling at the sour smell of stale whisky on the breath of this intruder who now bulked large and menacing in the dimly-lighted patio.

"I could say plenty about Manilla," the Rio Kid retorted.

Evidently the harsh note in the Rio Kid's voice brought caution to the big stranger, for he grunted deep in his throat.

"I'm Yankee Travers," he said slowly. "Manilla has worked for me. I've always found him reliable, so I don't like to hear a man speak ill of a friend."

The Rio Kid pushed Beth Price gently aside, his eyes fixed on Travers' bloated face, with the heavy jowls, the puffy eyes and rat-trap mouth, visible beneath the sweep of a stained mustache.

Before either of them could say more, a small

man, who came no higher than the. Rio Kid's shoulder, glided up from the shadows.

"Trouble, boss?" he asked the big man.

"No trouble, yet, Link."

The Rio Kid recalled this bantam gunman, Link Dant, who had been run out of Tucson and narrowly escaped hanging at Stockton. He was small, but so is a sidewinder, the Kid reflected. Dant had a reputation with guns and it was whispered that no one knew for sure just how many men he had killed. His dark eyes were never still and it seemed that he was looking everywhere at once.

It was interesting to know that this man who called himself "Yankee" Travers would have a bodyguard of Dant's caliber. Also interesting was the fact that Travers resented any slight to Rey Manilla.

"I will probably see you again, Captain Pryor," Travers said and turned on his heel to go into the house, Dant at his side.

The Rio Kid's eyes narrowed as he wondered how Travers had known his name.

"I despise that man," Beth Price whispered.

Bob Pryor questioned her about Travers. He was a wealthy landowner, who had made his riches by foreclosing on old Spanish ranchos. But many had forgotten the black chapter in his past. Now it was said that his power extended clear to the state capital at Sacramento. And as the girl revealed the last, Pryor was remembering what Fremont had said about the politically powerful figure who was giving orders to Manilla. Travers could very well be this man of mystery.

After promising Beth Price to do all he could in clearing Don Barling and locating her father, the Rio Kid left her with several young ladies who had found her in the patio. Quickly he rounded up Celestino, who had been enjoying the dance. The Mexican's happy grin faded when Pryor told him what had transpired in the patio.

"We keep our eyes on thees Senor Travers," Celestino whispered after the Rio Kid had pointed out the huge figure.

"Yeah, and I reckon this evening ain't goin' to be wasted after all," the Rio Kid said grimly.

CHAPTER VII

.

Death in the Morning

☐ Later that evening a group of men were discussing politics in one corner of the big room. While the others danced to the lilting music, the Rio Kid hovered near this group, keeping his ears open. He saw that Yankee Travers was doing more than his share of talking.

Now and then Pryor would find the man's baleful green eyes on him. Even that glance caused the hackles to rise at the back of the Kid's neck.

There was something cold and dangerous about this mountain of a man and what made him doubly dangerous was the friendship of the ever-present Link Dant at his side.

Antonio Coronel joined the group.

"What is California going to do with the thousands of unfortunate Chinese coolies now in our state?" Coronel asked.

Several of the men offered opinions, but it remained for Yankee Travers to put the match to the explosive subject.

"I have the perfect solution, gentlemen," he

66

volunteered. It was obvious that he was half-drunk on wine, for everytime a servant passed with a tray, he took a glass and downed it at a gulp. Now his green eyes were red-rimmed and there was a sneer on his lips.

"We should institute a system of slavery," Travers was bellowing. "I still say slavery is meant for some men. It's their lot in life."

There was a moment of shocked silence at Travers' words, then a buzz of talk. But it remained for Coronel to defy his influential guest.

"Sir, that is unthinkable," he declared. "Have you forgotten that a great war was fought to free the slaves?"

Travers snorted and took another glass of wine, his bloodshot eyes resting shrewdly on Coronel's flushed, angry face.

"The South had some good ideas, only we'll go 'em one better," he boasted. "Them coolies will make good slaves."

Antonio Coronel's gray head seemed to shake with anger. "Senor, today is Independence day, the anniversary of the birth of freedom. Do you not remember the principles we revere on this great day?"

"That's all right for that bunch in Washington," Travers snapped. "But California's three thousand miles away. We can all get rich off slave labor."

Coronel tried to argue, attempting to hold his

temper, for he was the host and, in his code, it was unthinkable to invite a man to his *casa* and then insult him.

Then Travers caught the Rio Kid's eye. "What's your view on the subject, Captain Pryor?" he asked, a note of prodding insolence in his voice.

Slowly the Rio Kid came away from the wall where he had been leaning, noticing that Travers' hand which held a wine glass did not tremble now. There was a cunning light in his green eyes and it was apparent to the Kid that Travers was not as drunk as he was pretending to be.

"I think that any man who wants to start slavery in this state or any other, is a traitor to his country!" the Rio Kid answered bluntly.

In the moment of shocked silence Anonio Coronel stared wide-eyed at the Kid. Link Dant looked as if he might draw a gun, but Travers gave a barely perceptible nod and the little gunman stepped aside. But his hands were near his gun belt.

Now Travers was moving swiftly, light on his feet as a dancer, in spite of his bulk. As the Rio Kid saw him approach, he dropped a hand to his gun, having no intention of getting caught in a cross-fire between Travers and his bodyguard. Travers pulled a glove from his pocket and slashed the ex-cavalry officer across the face with it. The Kid felt the sting, but did not flinch.

"I challenge you to a duel!" Travers bellowed. "If you've got any honor you'll meet me. Otherwise I'll hunt you down like a dog and kill you! No man can call me a traitor and live."

The Rio Kid had sensed all along that Travers had some plan in mind, therefore he was not too surprised at this turn of events.

"You name the place," he said coldly.

For a moment Travers was stilled, not expecting the Kid to accept so readily. Then he shook a fist under Pryor's nose.

"We meet in the river bed below the bridge," he growled. "At dawn?" He glanced questioningly at Pryor, who nodded in acceptance of the suggested hour.

Then he strode out of the house, Dant at his heels.

Antonio Coronel pulled the Rio Kid to one side, as the few men who had witnessed the challenge were excitedly discussing the forthcoming duel.

"I am sorry, senor, that this regrettable incident had to happen in my house," Coronel said. "Do not meet this Travers. He is a demon with the pistol."

"Thanks, Don Antonio," the Rio Kid answered. "But I reckon I can watch out for myself."

With a final word of reassurance to Beth Price, Pryor and Celestino took their leave of Coronel and left the *casa*.

"But General," Celestino said as they walked

rapidly toward the plaza, "you are not going to duel with this hombre."

"I'm goin' to call his bluff and see what kind of a corral he's tryin' to box me into," the Kid answered.

"I theenk I go along, too," Celestino declared, as he scanned both sides of the shadowy street.

They had gone but a block when the Rio Kid suddenly pulled Celestino into the darkened recess of a building entrance. Gun in hand, the Rio Kid stepped into a pool of moonlight and saw the figure of a man who evidently had been following them. As the stranger saw the gun in the Rio Kid's hand, he turned and fled, but Pryor had one glimpse of his face. He was Chinese. . . .

After a restless night spent in a hotel near the plaza, the Rio Kid and Celestino were up before dawn. The air was cold, the brush damp from the night fog, so that by the time they rode to the bluff that overlooked the dueling grounds in the river bottom, their pants legs were soaked.

"I do not like thees," Celestino whispered, as he peered ahead into the blackness.

"The fog'll lift soon," the Kid prophesied. "You stay up here on the bank. Keep your rifle handy and see that no skulker gets a shot at my back."

Celestino nodded, pulled his rifle from its saddle boot and dismounted. He tied his horse some distance from the bluff edge then crept forward on foot.

When Bob Pryor saw that Celestino had a good vantage point, the Rio Kid rode Saber down the slanting road that led to the river bed. Saber was frisky this morning and it was hard for the Kid to hold him in.

Almost as soon as Saber's hoofs touched dry sand, the sun shot up over the eastern hills, a red ball shining through the fog. In the brief light, the Kid saw a carriage pulled up ahead, its side-lamps still glowing.

Yankee Travers and Link Dant were there, also half a dozen other men who had been at the *baile* and witnessed the challenge. Pryor dismounted and tied Saber to a willow.

Travers hitched up the heavy gunbelt sloped around his paunch. "I didn't figure you'd come, Pryor," he said with a sly grin. "Did you make arrangements for buryin'? The county won't do it free, you know."

The Rio Kid matched his grin and jerked a thumb at Link Dant. "If there's goin' to be any duel, he's got to shuck his gun," he warned. "I don't hanker to get shot in the back."

For the first time the Rio Kid saw a flicker of indecision show in Travers' green eyes. The other men who had come to witness the duel agreed that Dant should discard his gun. Travers surprisingly agreed. Dant put his weapon in the

71

carriage and leaned against a rear wheel to glare at the tall, sunbronzed ex-cavalry officer.

"We ain't got no fancy duelin' pistols," Travers said. "I reckon six-guns oughta do the trick."

"Suits me," the Rio Kid agreed.

Again he noticed the indecision on Travers' face. The big man was plainly disturbed at the Rio Kid's self-confidence. Once he glanced up on the bluff, as if looking for someone.

A Los Angeles merchant named Meredith was going to do the counting. He was a perspiring little man who evidently wished he had stayed away.

"Ten paces," he said in a quavering vioce, "then fire."

"I'm ready," the Rio Kid said.

He cast a glance at the bluff where Celestino was hidden. Now the sun was up enough so that it dissolved the morning mists and he could plainly see the spot where his Mexican pard was crouched. But a little to the left he saw brush move and knew that someone was creeping forward.

There was no way to warn Celestino unless he called the whole thing off and that would ruin his purpose, which was to see Travers' hole card.

"Stand back to back, gentlemen," Meredith said in his quavering voice.

With a confident grin on his lips, the Rio Kid stepped around so that he would be walking toward the spot on the bluff where he had seen the brush move. Travers scowled at this, but said nothing. Now the Kid could feel Travers' broad back against his own shoulder blades as they lined up.

It was a tense moment, reflected in the drawn faces of the handful of witnesses who had gathered. Link Dant watched, his small, bony features expressionless.

Meredith began to count. "One—two—three—"

The Rio Kid started to walk, head down so that he could screen his gaze with his hatbrim. As he moved his blue eyes were fixed on that spot on the bluff where he had seen the brush move.

When Meredith reached the count of "six" there was a sudden flurryiin the brush. Pryor caught a glimpse of a bearded face and the reflection of sunlight on a rifle barrel. Acting instinctively, he side-stepped to bring up his gun in a dazzling blaze of speed, but it was unnecessary. There were two quick shots from Celestino's rifle up there on the bluff. The skulker's Winchester blasted a slug into the ground. Now the would-be attacker was plunging head-first over the bluff to land sprawling in the dust. He didn't move.

It all happened so quickly that Meredith and the other witnesses remained rooted to the spot. Yankee Travers had turned, but made no move toward the gun at his belt. There was incredulity in his green eyes as he stared at the ambusher's dead body.

Hardly had the echo of those shots blasted the morning stillness than the Rio Kid spotted action on the opposite bluff. Another rifleman, dressed in trailworn denims, was on his feet, firing back at someone deep in the brush. Then he swung around to bring his rifle to bear on Bob Pryor, standing alone down there in the dry river bed.

Again it was instinct that caused the Rio Kid to drop suddenly to the ground, yanking those twin sixes from holster leather as he fell. The denim clad hombre's slug creased the air above his head. Then those famous Colts were rolling shots up to the bluff.

Battered from the Rio Kid's lead, the ambusher pitched forward on his face to hang on the lip of the bluff, a crimson splotch showing on an expanse of gypsum below, an ever-widening red stain.

Hardly had the man fallen than those in the river bed saw a black-clad figure spring out of the brush and go racing off toward the back country. The Kid had a brief glimpse of the man —a Chinese. It was the same man who had followed him and Celestino the night before.

"Looks like that Chinese was tryin' to kill the skulker for me," the Rio Kid said, giving Yankee Travers a level look. "Good thing he was up there and able to drive the hombre into the open where I could level my guns on him."

Travers blustered, eying the twin guns the Rio Kid still held in his hand. A film of sweat showed at the edge of his mustache beneath that great beak of a nose.

"Those men were trying to kill me!" he cried.

Captain Bob Pryor, the Rio Kid, laughed in his face. "That was your little scheme to have me murdered," he said. "You figgered I'd be an easy mark for them skulkers because I'd have my mind on the duel."

"I never saw either of those men in my life," Travers said indignantly.

By now Celestino had ridden down into the river bottom to sit his horse a few feet behind the carriage where he could keep an eye on Link Dant. The bantam gunman was strapping on his gunbelt again.

Meredith, the storekeeper, was plainly upset. He and the other witnesses wanted no more of dueling. They caught up their horses and galloped off toward town, having enough bloodshed for one day.

Without a word, Yankee Travers climbed into his fancy buggy and was driven by Link Dant up the slanting road toward Los Angeles. The man's puffy face was pale and he seemed shaken by the events of the morning.

After inspecting the dead men, the Rio Kid and Celestino rode away from the scene of death.

"They're probably a couple of gents that

Travers hired on the spur of the moment for his dirty work," the Kid said.

"What about thees Chinaman?" Celestino asked later when they were eating a hurried breakfast.

Pryor shrugged, scowling as he blew on his coffee. He was trying to figure where the Oriental fitted into this business. It was plain that the Chinese had either attempted to kill Travers' ambusher, or force him into the open where he would be under the Rio Kid's eyes.

"We're goin' to have a look at Chinatown," the Kid said grimly, as he and Celestino left the cafe. "I'd know that hombre if I ever saw him again."

CHAPTER VIII

Chinatown

☐ Generally speaking, the Chinese quarter of Los Angeles, at this time, consisted of two streets, lined with shops and living quarters east of the plaza. Black-clad Chinese shuffled by on both sides of the alley-like street where the Rio Kid and Celestino were walking, and from the sidelong glances cast in their direction, they knew they were unwelcome. There was a tension here that Pryor could almost feel.

They loitered along the street, looking into windows full of Oriental curios. Pig-tailed Chinese worked with their heavy irons at a laundry, eyeing Celestino and the Kid with suspicion.

The Chinese were polite when the pair entered shops, but there was a definite coolness. The Kid knew this was alien, for he had spent some time in San Francisco and knew the Chinese were a friendly race.

It seemed as if these yellow men realized they were becoming the pawns for power in California. There had been trouble in the northern part of the state and any moment the violence might shift here. So it was small wonder they were suspicious.

"It does not look like we find heem," Celestino finally admitted after they had trudged the short blocks of the Oriental quarter.

"I reckon our friend has hit the trail," Pryor agreed.

Just as they were about to give up the search and head east for Searles' Marsh, as General Fremont has suggested, the Rio Kid gripped Celestino's arm.

"Look up ahead," he whispered, indicating a lone Chinese placidly smoking before a small shop.

The Mexican grew tense. "That is the one, General," he said in a low voice.

As the Rio Kid and Celestino approached, the Chinese calmly turned and strolled into the shop.

"You theenk thees might be the trap?" Celestino asked suspiciously.

"I don't think so," Pryor said with a shake of his head. "But we're goin' in anyhow."

The interior of the shop was dimly lighted and for a moment they were nearly blind as they stepped out of the bright sun glare of the dusty street. They halted just inside the door, conscious of the sweetish odor of incense in the air. Now the Rio Kid could make out a bronze Chinese god on a teakwood pedestal.

"Welcome, Captain Pryor," the Oriental said

gravely. He stood behind the counter and bowed slightly from the waist.

"How'd you know my name?" the Rio Kid asked, wondering at the almost perfect English spoken by this Oriental stranger.

"We have a mutual friend," the Chinese answered, an ironic smile on his lips.

The Rio Kid and Celestino had walked to the counter. Now they waited for an explanation, both studying the bland face of the Oriental.

"I am Chang Lee, son of the slain Chang Wah," the Chinese admitted.

"Lieutenant Barling's friend!" the Kid exclaimed.

With a nod of his head Chang Lee indicated they were to follow. He opened a small door behind the counter and disappeared. Hands on gun butts the Rio Kid and Celestino followed. They found themselves in a small dimly-lighted room. The furnishings were simple. A charcoal stove, two chairs and a table. An unlighted candle was stuck in the neck of a wine bottle, while windows were covered with heavy drapes. The rear door was heavily barred. This was certainly not the usual type of room to be found behind a Chinese shop, the Rio Kid reflected.

"How'd you know about me?" Pryor asked Chang Lee suspiciously.

"I was concealed in the patio at the home of the most honorable Don Antonio," he explained.

"I heard you talking about Lieutenant Barling to Beth Price, the schoolteacher."

"And you followed us out of town last night," the Rio Kid snapped.

"I wanted to speak to you then," Chang Lee replied. "And I overheard the duel proposed by that dog of all dogs, Yankee Travers. That night I trailed Travers and heard him make plans to have two men at the dueling grounds to kill you."

The Rio Kid grinned. "You sure proved yourself an hombre with plenty of nerve," he said, a note of admiration in his voice.

"It remained for your own skill to dispose of the assassin," Chang Lee replied modestly.

Now that Pryor could see him in a better light it was evident that Chang Lee was a high-caste Chinese. His almond eyes were level, direct. His features were delicate, yet an underlying strength gave character to his face. Now he was dressed in Mandarin silks with a round black cap upon his head.

Now the Rio Kid and Celestino were sitting in the chair the Chinaman had indicated. Pryor was scowling for he did not know how to bring up the murder of Chang Lee's father. But it had to be done, for he felt in that way he could help clear Barling.

"You know about your father?" Pryor asked softly, watching Chang Lee's face.

"My father went north, disguised as a poor

81

traveler," Chang Lee answered. "He wanted to see our old friend, Lieutenant Barling, for he is of the military."

"And Chang Wah thought Barling could get the Army after the men who are persecutin' your people?" the Kid guessed and knew his assumption was correct for Chang Lee nodded.

"I did not know my father had gone until it was too late to stop him," Chang Lee continued. "Friends told me. In some manner a man who calls himself Rey Manilla followed. This man murdered my father and put the blame on my old friend, Don Barling."

The Kid saw the grief that sprang into those almond eyes. "I reckon you've got a way of puttin' it in your own language," he said, "but I'll say it in English. I'm goin' to see that Manilla pays for that cold-blooded murder."

"English will do very well," Chang Lee replied. "I think in your language almost as well as I do my own. Missionaries taught me in Pekin before my father and I came to your country."

The the Rio Kid and Celestino exchanged glances as if the same thought had struck them both simultaneously.

"How come you knew all about Manilla and the murder of your father?" Pryor said sharply. "Barling couldn't have written because he told me he didn't even know where you was."

For the first time Chang Lee's almond eyes narrowed and he drew himself stiffly erect in his silken robes as he stood there in the center of the small room staring at the Rio Kid.

"Captain Pryor," he said after a moment, "I am going to ask you a question. Do you believe army courts to be infallible?"

Wondering at this strange question, the Rio Kid looked up at Chang Lee a long moment before replying. Inside his brain were many puzzling thoughts and he had a hunch that a lot might depend on the kind of an answer he gave.

"If you're talkin' about Lieutenant Barling," he said slowly, "I don't figger he's guilty—and I never did."

Still Chang Lee's yellow features were immobile. "Captain Pryor, would you condone escape from military justice?" the Oriental went on.

A sudden fear leaped through the Rio Kid like flame. "Barling!" he cried. "Did he try to escape?"

"Yes."

"If he killed anybody makin' that break, they'll hang him," the Rio Kid snapped.

"He killed no one, Captain," Chang Lee said with an inscrutable smile. "I am glad you feel as you do."

With a rustle of silk he padded to the rear door, lifted the bar out of its slot and opened the portal. A muddy, red-eyed figure strode into the room. It was Lieutenant Don Barling, who by now should be arriving on Alcatraz Island to begin serving a life sentence for murder.

CHAPTER IX

The Search

☐ Shaken by emotion, Barling stood in the center of the room, then leaped forward to grasp the Kid's hand in his own, muttering his name through stiffened lips as if in prayer. Chang Lee barred the door again.

"He came to me last evening," Chang Lee explained. "One of my countrymen directed him to my shop."

"What happened?" the Rio Kid demanded of the officer. "Lieutenant Michaels. Did you—"

"I tricked him," Barling said and sank wearily into a chair. "It was easy to fool a man like him, who had his head crammed with West Point theory. It seems the text books don't cover a situation like this. I made my break at night. The men did not try too hard to cut me down. I rather suspect they fired over my head."

It was evident that Lieutenant Barling had been in mad flight since his break from the Army escort. Somewhere on the trip to Los Angeles, he had discarded his uniform. Now he wore faded levis, a torn cotton shirt and an old sweat-stained hat. He did not explain what had happened to his uniform and the Rio Kid did not ask.

"I hardly ate or slept," Barling explained. "My one thought was to get to Los Angeles. I knew you were coming here and I hoped I could find Chang Lee somewhere, too. It was sheer luck that I found you both."

"The next thing is to keep out of the Army's way," Bob Pryor said thoughtfully. "Did Michaels trail you?"

"I don't know," Barling replied. "I suppose he has picked up my trail by this time. He'd like nothing better than to see me hanged."

"We've got to be careful or he may get his chance," the Rio Kid said grimly.

Barling began to pace the floor. "I've got to see Beth," he said suddenly. "I can't stand it that she doesn't know how things are!"

A wild look swept into the officer's bloodshot eyes and the Rio Kid pushed him gently back into a chair. Quickly he told of the meeting with Beth Price and the disappearance of her father.

"The main thing you've got to do is stay out of sight!" the Rio Kid advised. "No tellin' where Michaels will look."

Celestino snapped his fingers. "We go to see the Senor John Searles, no?" he said quickly. "We can take theese Barling weeth us."

"I thought of that," the Rio Kid admitted. "But it ain't as easy as it sounds. I figger we ought to stay right here for now. We know that Yankee Travers is in with Manilla. Travers is in town so it's possible Manilla is around somewheres, too."

"Where we go?" Celestino asked as he saw the Rio Kid head for the door.

"I hanker to have a showdown with Manilla," Pryor snapped. "We ought to finish this whole thing right here and now."

Barling was plainly eager to join the pair. "I want to get in on this," he exclaimed. "I figure Manilla has got to die a thousand times for killing Chang Wah."

As he said the last a shadow of sorrow crossed Chang Lee's almond eyes at mention of his father's death. But instantly it was gone. He and Barling agreed to accept the Rio Kid's leadership and follow his first order by staying in the shop.

"Somebody might see you," Pyror warned Barling. "Stay under cover till dark."

Making sure they were unobserved, the Rio Kid and Celestino slipped out of the shop and made their way down the street toward the plaza. The day was almost unbearably hot and perspiration began to work it's way across the Kid's bronzed face.

"First we're huntin' up Beth Price," the Rio Kid said, as they swung past the Pico House where Fremont had stayed.

"But why not see Travers first?" Celestino

asked, as they threaded their way through the crowd on the boardwalk.

"We got to tell her Barling's escaped," the Kid said quickly. "She's got a level head. She'll send a note back to Barling, tellin' him it ain't wise for 'em to meet now."

They crossed dusty Fort Street, dodged a freight wagon and reached the opposite boardwalk. "Why do you not want them to see each other?" Celestino asked, his Latin romantic nature rebelling at the thought of keeping Barling and his fiancee apart.

"Can't take any chances, that's all," the Rio Kid replied. "If Lieutenant Michaels comes here, Barling will never live to get to Alcatraz Island. That's my hunch."

At the schoolhouse they learned from a prim teacher that Beth Price had not come to teach her classes today. After obtaining her address, they cut down a few blocks where the stores were replaced by homes. One of these was Mrs. Hudspeth's Boarding House where Beth Price resided.

Just inside the white picket fence were half a dozen orange trees. It was lucky that these shielded the Rio Kid and Celestino from the house for, just as they were about to turn in at the gate, they heard voices.

Gripping Celestino's arm, Pryor pulled him in back of a buggy which was at the walk. Celestino whistled in surprise as he followed the Kid's pointing finger and saw blue-clad soldiers on the rooming house porch.

An officer was talking to a gray-haired woman who appeared to be Mrs. Hudspeth. The officer was Lieutenant John Michaels. His uniform was not so natty now. It was dusty and, even from this distance, the Rio Kid could see that he was thoroughly angry.

"I'm sorry," Mrs. Hudspeth said, her voice carrying to them. "Miss Price is not here. She took the early stage for Indian Wells."

"Was anybody with her?" the lieutenant asked quickly and gave a brief description of Don Barling. But the woman claimed she had seen no one answering that description.

"Her father's been missin'," Mrs. Hudspeth continued. "I reckon she went up there to look for him."

The Rio Kid and Celestino watched the lieutenant and his five troopers walk around the corner where their horses were tied, mount and ride off.

"What do you make of the senorita going to find her *padre*?" Celestino asked, as they walked rapidly back the way they had come.

"I wish she hadn't done that," the Kid answered grimly. "That part of the country ain't no place for a woman like Beth Price."

Keeping to the crowded sections of the boardwalk so as to lessen the risk of being spotted by

Lieutenant Michaels and his troopers, the Kid and Celestino made a quick visit to the Pico House. Pryor wanted to check up on Yankee Travers to see if the rich landowner was still in town. It was Antonio Coronel who had told him this was Travers' town residence.

But the clerk informed them that Travers had left that morning.

"I got business with him," Pryor told the clerk. "Got any idea where he went?"

The clerk eyed the tall blue-eyed man with the yellow hat and army tunic. He gave a moment to regard the twin sixes holstered at his lean waist.

"Mr. Travers' destination was Indian Wells," the clerk replied after a moment. "He took the morning stage."

Outside, the Kid and Celestino held a brief consultation. There was no telling what might happen to Beth Price, for it was apparent that she was on the same stage with Travers. If she asked indiscreet questions about her father, she might invite trouble.

"She should've stayed put like I told her," the Rio Kid said as they stood for a moment just outside the crowded hotel scanning the street.

"That ees the trouble weeth some women," the Mexican put it with a sly grin. "They theenk weeth the heart instead of the head."

Now that Don Barling had escaped, their troubles were intensified. Added to the disappearance of Beth Price, it doubled their danger. It would have been a herculean task in itself to track down Rey Manilla and bring him to justice. But now it was more complicated. They had to make sure that Barling was not recaptured before he had a chance to clear his name.

As they rounded the far corner of the hotel they saw the five troopers just dismounting at the plaza, tying their horses to a picket fence. But Lieutenant Michaels was not in sight. There was a possibility that the troopers might recognize them as having been visitors at Fort Tejon, so the Rio Kid and Celestino skirted the plaza while the soldiers lounged on a grassy plot.

"I don't trust Michaels," the Rio Kid said as they entered the alley-like street where Chang Lee's shop was situated. "I'd sure like to know where he is right now."

Half expecting to see Michaels inside the shop, they carefully peered into the front window before entering. But there was no one inside. In the little room behind the shop they confronted Barling and Chang Lee.

"Did you see Beth?" Barling demanded.

"She's taken the stage for Indian Wells to look for her father," the Rio Kid said bluntly.

"Then she doesn't know I'm free!"

Quickly the Rio Kid told of seeing Lieutenant Michaels and the troopers. "Our plans have got to be changed," he finished. "I reckon we ought to head for Indian Wells, pronto. Beth was on the same stage with Travers."

Barling's teeth were clenched so hard that his jaw muscles ribbed out on either side and there was a wild look in his pale eyes. The young ex-lieutenant's explosive temper was boiling to the surface.

"If they lay a hand on Beth, I'll fix 'em!"

He started to rush out the back door and the Rio Kid had to restrain him forcibly.

"Won't do no good to lose your head," he warned. "If Michaels spots you, I reckon you'll never have to worry about seein' Beth again."

Those grim words seemed to sober Barling somewhat. He shook himself free of the Rio Kid's strong fingers.

"You lead the way," he said breathing heavily. "What do we do next?"

Pryor wasted no words. "Chang Lee, I see you've gotten a gun for Barling," he said. "Can you do as well with two horses?"

Chang Lee allowed a brief smile to play across his lips. "I have anticipated your order," he said gravely. "Two of my countrymen have arranged for fast horses. They are waiting not a block from here."

The Rio Kid nodded, noting for the first time that Chang Lee had shed his Mandarin silks and now wore a black hat, black shirt, pants and boots. It was the same outfit he had worn that morning when he interfered with Yankee Travers' plan for ambush.

"Are you ridin' with us?" the Kid asked him.

"That country is where so many of my countrymen are disappearing," Chang Lee answered. "I believe that somewhere in that vicinity we will find the answer to our problem."

"I got a hunch you're right," the Rio Kid told him.

"Are we leaving now?" Barling asked, his face lighting with anticipation.

"You and Chang Lee leave together," Bob Pryor ordered. "Me'n Celestino will meet you at Workman. It's a stage stop about five miles east of town. There's some pepper trees in back. Stay behind those till me and Celestino get there."

The men shook hands all around. "Don't take any chances," the Rio Kid warned in parting, as he and Celestino left.

Then they slipped out of the shop and quickly got out of the Chinese district, to head for the stable where they had left their horses.

CHAPTER X

Trapped

☐ Five or six troopers still lounged at the far side of the plaza, but Lieutenant Michaels still had not returned. Celestino and the Rio Kid entered the wide stable doorway and stepped into the gloom with its stamping horses, the smells of hay and sweat and fresh droppings. The fat stableman sat in his office, feet on his desk. Even from that distance they could see that his face was pale. He watched them enter but made no move to rise, and the Kid's sixth sense began to work as he saw the stableman's wide, staring eyes. The man was wetting his lips now.

A thin thread of tension flashed along the Rio Kid's nerves. Up ahead he saw Saber and Celestino's pinto in adjoining stalls. Celestino seemed to sense the unseen danger, too, for he slowed his pace.

Now their eyes were becoming accustomed to the gloom. Just as the Kid was about to turn so his back would be to the wall, a commanding voice cut out of the shadows behind a pile of sacked grain.

"Get your hands up, Pryor! You, too, Mireles! You are both under arrest for aiding and abetting in the escape of a U.S. Army prisoner!" The voice had come from behind them and the Rio Kid recognized it as belonging to Lieutenant Michaels. He had evidently been hiding there to cover them when they entered. The stableman had known he was there, but was powerless to interfere with an Army arrest.

Hands raised shoulder high, the Rio Kid and Celestino turned slowly. The Mexican, always taking his cues from Pryor, showed no signs of fight. Under other circumstances the Rio Kid might have tried to shoot his way out of the trap, but he had no wish to fight an Army officer and run the risk of killing the man. He had little use for Michaels but, after all, he did wear the blue of a U.S. Army lieutenant.

Michaels did not look as polished as he had that day at Fort Tejon. Now his face was haggard, his uniform unpressed and his boots caked with mud, but he still had a certain underlying dignity.

"How did you find us?" the Rio Kid asked, stalling for time, his mind busy with thoughts of escape.

"I checked the stables," Michaels answered with a cold smile, as he stepped into view, a cocked Army revolver in his hand. "I would never forget your horse, Captain Pryor."

Celestino had uttered no word. His olive skin was stretched tight across his cheekbones, his lips a firm line. He stood there on the balls of his feet, his reflexes ready to snap a hand gunward if Pryor gave the signal.

"You got no authority to hold a gun on us," Pryor reminded the lieutenant.

"You helped Barling escape!" Michaels shouted.

"So Barling has escaped," the Rio Kid answered, evading a trap he knew Michaels had set for him.

"I see you won't admit you knew that," the lieutenant said. "That will come in time. Now I'll call my troopers and have you escorted to jail and then continue the search for Barling. I'm sure he's in Los Angeles and I intend to find him. Next time I'll have the pleasure of escorting all three of you to Alcatraz Island."

The Rio Kid knew that once the troopers were called they would have no chance. Now was the time to act. He stiffened and he noted that Celestino shot him a sidelong glance, as if to anticipate his thoughts.

"I dispersed my troops in plain sight," Michaels said, evidently proud of his strategy. "I intended to give you a false sense of security and it worked. You see, Pryor, the Academy makes an officer. You and Barling did not have that privilege, therefore I have an unfair advantage over you."

There was a mocking note in the lieutenant's voice. He was about to turn and yell for his troopers. That was the moment the Rio kid counted on. Before Michaels could execute his intention, a figure entered the wide doorway—a tall, knife-faced man, dressed in the black silks of a Chinese merchant.

When he saw the Rio Kid and Celestino with their hands up, a vicious smile of triumph stretched his lips into a grimace.

"Good work, Michaels," the man said and pulled a big six-shooter from beneath his black shirt.

Now that he had come to stand beside the lieutenant in the light, Pryor could see it was Rey Manilla. Anger boiled up inside him when he saw the man who had murdered Chang Lee's father and had framed Barling for the crime. And thoughts of the hapless Chinese who were victims of his greed only added fuel to that anger.

Michaels quickly told Manilla how he had captured the Rio Kid and Celestino.

Manilla laughed, cocking the big gun in his hand, his yellow eyes lighted with pleasure.

"My ability to speak Chinese has its points," he said, talking to the lieutenant, but keeping an eye on Pryor and the Mexican. "The stupid Chinese merchants did not see through my disguise. It was easy to prove I was working with Chang Lee to bring the hated Rey Manilla to justice." He laughed again.

"What did you learn about Barling?" Michaels demanded, never taking his eyes from his prisoners.

"I learned a lot," Manilla snapped and noted with satisfaction that the Rio Kid and Celestino had stiffened at his words. "Barling and Chang Lee left Chinatown not ten minutes ago, riding east along the stage road. I imagine you can get your prisoner easily."

Michaels was overjoyed. "Good work!" he cried. "Soon as I take these prisoners to jail, we'll ride and get Barling."

'Let me and my men take Pryor and Mireles," Manilla suggested craftily. "You don't want to lose any time."

For a moment the lieutenant weighed the wisdom of this. "Don't trust these two alone," he said finally. "Are your men nearby?"

For an answer Manilla turned and whistled. Instantly three heavily armed gunmen stepped into the stable.

"My men are never far away," Manilla explained.

Pryor noticed that one of the men was black-haired Mike Jarel, still clad in his greasy buckskins. He had been with Manilla at Fort Tejon.

"You take over these men," the lieutenant ordered. "But see that they are not harmed. They must be treated as Army prisoners."

"Don't worry about that," Manilla said quickly.

And for the first time the Rio Kid began to get a clue to John Michaels' character. He wondered if perhaps the young officer was merely overzealous and not in league with Manilla, after all.

Michaels had the natural suspicion of most Academy men toward officers who had risen from the ranks, hence his ready acceptance of Barling's guilt and the assumption that Pryor and Celestino had helped some way in the escape. His vanity would not let him believe that Barling could have made the break unaided.

Guns of Manilla's three men were brought to bear on the Rio kid and Celestino. Inside the small office, the stableman had taken his feet off the desk now and stood up. He was definitely wanting no part of this trouble, but watched silently from the doorway.

Lieutenant Michaels had holstered his gun and was now running toward the plaza, shouting at his troopers. Men on the boardwalk turned to stare as the soldiers quickly mounted and came spurring forward, leading the lieutenant's horse. Quickly Michaels was in the saddle, leading his detail out of town at full gallop to capture the elusive ex-lieutenant, Don Barling.

The Rio Kid knew he might succeed. Chang Lee and Barling would be waiting at the stage station. Perhaps they could make a fight of it, but they would be outnumbered. And the old fear returned, as he stood there under the guns of Manilla and his men. If one of the troopers was killed, Barling would very likely never be able to clear his record.

After all, the troopers were merely following orders. The War Department would take the view that Barling should never have tried to escape, that the wheels of Army justice would have turned and eventually have brought about his freedom.

Manilla seemed to be reading Pryor's thoughts, for he grinned.

"It looks like your little game is over," he said in that peculiar sing-song voice. "Saddle your horses. We're going to make sure you never have *another* game, Pryor!"

CHAPTER XI

"Run for it!"

☐ Without a word the Rio Kid and Celestino walked to their mounts, Manilla and his men fanning out across the stable so as to have them constantly under their guns. It was plain to the Kid that Manilla had no intention of taking them to jail. They would be taken out and shot. Manilla would then be able to tell Michaels that they had tried to escape. It was all very simple.

As they reached for their saddles on the pegs, Pryor had a second to whisper encouragement to Celestino.

"Watch me," he murmured. "We've got to make the break in here."

Used to danger as they were, they went about the business of saddling with no outward show of emotions. So far they had not been disarmed and that in itself was a break. For Manilla probably figured to let them get into the saddle and then shoot them down.

As if echoing the Rio Kid's thoughts, Manilla turned and yelled an order at the stableman.

"Go out and buy yourself a drink!" he snapped.

The stableman hesitated. "But I got to stay here."

"Buy that drink!" Manilla's voice had a flat, ugly edge.

The fat stableman left and Pryor saw him ambling along the boardwalk, glancing back once.

"We don't want any witnesses, do we, Pryor?" Manilla purred. "Now get into the saddles! Both of you!"

It was plain what he intended to do. He would let them ride toward the door. Then they would be shot to death. The horses would stampede in the excitement and Manilla's story would be accepted by the law. Two military prisoners had tried to make a break for the open and had died in the attempt.

Saber snorted and pawed the ground. That black stripe which ran down his back began to quiver and the Kid knew that the war horse sensed the danger.

He had just backed Saber out of the stall when he suddenly smote the dun on the rump with the flat of his hand. The Kid jumped back into the shelter of the stall, yelling for Celestino to follow suit.

Guns had opened up from Manilla and his men, who were forced to leap aside in order to escape the two plunging horses. Saber was hurtling out into the middle of the stable, yellow teeth bared. The Rio Kid deliberately showed himself, to draw fire away from the two horses.

As bullets came his way, he dropped the hammers of his sixes. One of Manilla's men doubled up and pitched forward on his face, guns exploding into the ground.

Manilla stepped aside from Celestino's pinto, raised his guns to bear on the Rio Kid. At that instant an avalanche of frenzied horseflesh bore down on him. Saber trumpeted, eyes dilated, to raise on his hind legs, forefeet pawing the air. Manilla threw himself to one side and had to roll over and over, dropping his guns in order to keep from being smashed by those heavy hoofs.

Celestino's lead snapped a gunman upright against the far wall. The man stood rigid for a moment, then collapsed. Mike Jarel dived into an empty stall to escape the withering fire from the guns of the Rio Kid and Celestino.

There were shouts from the street as men raced toward the stable.

"Let's make a run for it!" the Rio Kid cried as he vaulted into the saddle.

Celestino had his pinto's reins and now he hit leather and followed Pryor's lead through the doorway.

As the Rio Kid gave the spurs to Saber, he caught a glimpse of Manilla trying to retrieve his weapons. But he held his fire, for it was against his code to shoot down an unarmed man.

Shots from Mike Jarel's gun whistled over their heads as they cleared the stable. Now the crowd split in two as the horsemen raced toward them. There was a mad scramble to escape these demons on horseback. Somebody fired a rifle at them, but the shot went wild. Manilla's strident voice came to them dimly as they skirted Chinatown and raced out the east road.

Letting Saber have his head, the Rio Kid led them in a mad gallop down the dusty road. He was thankful that previous trips to this area had given him a fair layout of the town and the surrounding country. He prayed that Lieutenant Michaels, on his way to capture Barling, had no such knowledge.

The stage road wound through a Mexican village on the eastern bank of the dry river but the Kid knew by climbing a low bank of hills to the north he would be able to save at least three miles.

"They are coming, General!" Celestino shouted, pointing back toward town.

"Let 'em come," the Rio Kid said with a tight grin as he sent Saber plunging up the hillside.

Pursuit had been quickly organized, for a body of horsemen was sweeping out of town in their wake. In all probability the riders did not know why they were giving chase. But a sleepy town like Los Angeles did not afford too much excitement and saloon hangers-on welcomed any chance to ride. This was giving vent to their pent-up energy, wasting ammunition by firing at the fleeing pair.

"That was a close one!" Celestino cried. "I thought thees Manilla had us!"

The Rio Kid glanced back and saw that his hard-riding companion was grinning broadly.

He and Celestino thrived on excitement. It made their nerves tingle to outwit a man like Rey Manilla, but they both realized that it was only a temporary victory at best. Manilla would stop at nothing to see them killed. He had underestimated the resourcefulness of the two frontiersmen, but he would not do so again. If Manilla did not dispose of them this time, the whole diabolical scheme fostered by Yankee Travers would come tumbling down around his shoulders.

Praying that they were not too late to save Barling and Chang Lee, Pryor led the way across the ridge and down the other side. Now they could see the stage station and the grove of pepper trees behind it, but off to the left was a rising dust cloud and the Kid saw the flash of sabers in the sunlight. Lieutenant Michaels and his troopers were moving up fast.

"Senor Barling and Chang Lee!" Celestino shouted, pointing at the two men beside the horses in the grove. "They see us!"

The Rio Kid began to wave his arm wildly, indicating to the pair that they should ride. The two men seemed to sense trouble, for now they were in saddles. As the Rio Kid and Celestino swept down the slope, Barling and Chang Lee fell in beside them. Soon they were galloping stirrup to stirrup.

"What happened?" Barling demanded.

"Michaels!" the Rio Kid shouted, and jerked his head in the direction of the advancing troopers.

Michaels had evidently spotted them for now his men were firing. Those troopers were excellent shots and bullets began to land uncomfortably close but the Rio Kid refused to return the fire. After all, those were U.S. cavalrymen. Pryor knew the only chance they had lay in outmaneuvering the troopers.

The chase led for another five miles by Pryor and his friends, was beginning to tell on the horses. Saber and Celestino's pinto were becoming winded at the fast pace, for they had traveled at a dead run from town. Of course, the Army horses would fare no better, but Michaels might push his mounts to the extreme and the Kid was not willing to do that. It was easy to ruin a good horse and he was taking no chances with Saber.

Now they were galloping across an expanse of sand, their horses hoofs churning up a great cloud of dust. As the Rio Kid glanced back he saw that the troopers were screened by the dust cloud. That could work both ways, he reasoned.

As they swept close to the hills, he suddenly gave an order and they turned left into a canyon, grown high with oaks. There they sat their winded horses, sheltered from the flats by a protecting shoulder of rock. They could hear the pound of the cavalry horses as they swept on past.

"I reckon we got rid of 'em for a while," the Rio Kid said. "And it looks like the bunch from town have given up the chase. We'll cut north and hit the trail for Indian Wells. Michaels ought to have himself some fun tryin' to track us through these mountains."

It was pretty obvious that Rey Manilla knew their destination would be Indian Wells, for he was undoubtedly aware of the fact that Beth Price had gone there. He would know that Barling would waste no time in trying to reach the girl.

"Where you theenk Manilla has gone, General?" Celestino asked as they rode slowly deeper into the canyon.

"I figure he'll be cuttin' over to Indian Wells," the Rio Kid answered, giving voice to his thoughts. "We'll probably tie into him there. But we can't take the regular road on account of Michaels. We'll have to take the long way."

It did not take the Rio Kid long to tell Don Barling and Chang Lee of the encounter with Michaels and of the narrow escape from Manilla's men.

Barling cast an anxious glance over his shoulder, but no one was on their back trail. His

110

concern was not for his own safety, the Rio Kid realized. He was worrying about Beth Price and her foolish plan to travel into the desert in the heart of the renegade country to find her father.

"I don't want Michaels to catch up to me now," Barling admitted as they climbed a zig-zag trail. "Later I'll welcome a chance to fight him, but not now."

They were moving up into high country, where pines seemed to grow out of the solid rock walls that hemmed them in.

It appeared to be a blind canyon, but the Rio Kid knew this led out onto the desert on the other side of the mountains. He had been through here once before when a friend was cutting timber on contract for the Army.

"I reckon we're safe unless one of them troopers was in Los Angeles when the Army was cuttin' logs up here," the Rio Kid said. "He might remember this place."

"How soon we get to Indian Wells?" Celestino wanted to know.

"First we'll have a pow wow with John Searles," the Rio Kid said grimly. "Remember that Fremont said Searles had a good idea of what was goin' on back in the mountains."

"I hope he can give me some news of my missing countrymen," Chang Lee put in.

Although he had never been there, the Rio Kid knew the general direction of Indian Wells. His uncanny sense of direction, fostered after years on the danger trails of the West, enabled him to have a reasonably accurate idea of his location at all times. Now he intended to make camp just the other side of the mountains and proceed directly across the desert to Searles' Marsh.

"*Amigos*, from here on in we've got to keep our guns ready," the Rio Kid warned, "'cause we're gittin' in Yankee Travers' territory."

CHAPTER XII

Searles' Marsh

☐ It was two days later that the weary party of riders finally emerged from the sagebrush and sand, not far from the cluster of wooden buildings beside the dry lake known as Searles' Marsh. Dusty, tired, their horses blowing, the quartet moved slowly down a slanting hill toward the main building.

In spite of the grueling miles, Saber was still ready to travel, a contrast to the weary horses of Chang Lee and Barling. Celestino's pinto had held up nearly as well as Saber, but it was clear that the Chinaman and Barling would have to have fresh mounts before they could proceed.

Raw sunlight glistened on the salt and trona crystals that coated the huge dry lake. Near the edge was the apparatus that John Searles used to extract borax from the briny crust of the lake.

A couple of Searles's workers lounged in chairs under the wooden awning of the main building. They told the quartet where they could put up their horses.

"John Searles is in the main buildin', goin' over the books," one of the men volunteered.

Leaving Celestino and the others to care for the horses, Bob Pryor entered the building. Inside was a collection of odds and ends, rope, cable single jacks and drills. It was beyond a pile of crated machinery that the Rio Kid found John Searles working at a roll top desk.

"You're John Searles," the Rio Kid said and extended his hand. "General Fremont told me to look you up."

At mention of the famous frontiersman, Searles was on his feet, grasping the Rio Kid's hand.

"Any friend of Fremont's is sure a friend of mine," he exclaimed.

Searles pulled up a chair and the Kid sat down. This friend of General Fremont's was an imposing figure, tall, with his hair worn long and a neatly trimmed beard adorning a strong face.

Former bear hunter and Indian fighter, Searles had the vision of a pioneer. It was a decade before that he had first seen the crystals beside the dry lake here and realized their value. But it wasn't until several years later that he was able to return here and put his plant in operation. He had found a borax deposit worth many times the value of the average gold claim.

His shrewd eyes took in the Rio Kid's dusty clothes, his sweat-stained face and his piercing blue eyes.

"You're eatin' with me and the boys tonight," he said.

When the Rio Kid told him of the others in his party, Searles, with typical Western hospitality, included them also.

Without bothering with preliminaries, the Rio Kid told of his meeting with Fremont and how the general had recited his story of the diabolical plot against the Chinese of California. While Pryor talked, the famous frontiersman leaned back in his swivel chair, staring out the window at the jagged blue peaks of the Sierras in the distance.

"Too bad Fremont isn't staying in California," Searles muttered when the Rio Kid had told him of the general's appointment as governor of Arizona Territory. "Fremont's needed here. If somethin' isn't done pronto, there's goin' to be trouble."

"I've got a hunch that Indian Wells is the hub of the whole mess," Bob Pryor said.

"I've figured for a long time that Rey Manilla's headquarters is around there someplace," Searles added.

"Any idea of the location of his headquarters?" the Rio Kid asked.

Searles fingered his beard thoughtfully a moment before answering. "That's goin' to take a heap of doin'," he finally said, "tryin' to find Manilla's hangout. I've seen wagon loads of Chinese goin' through here. But I ain't never seen one of 'em come out."

"Any idea where they go?" the Rio Kid asked,

his lips tightening as he realized the seeming impossibilities of his task.

Searles shook his head. "I been in Indian Wells, but I ain't seen many Chinese there," he admitted, "outside of maybe two or three at a time."

"That means that Manilla has his hideout in the mountains north of here," the Kid said, indicating the blue ridges they could see through the window, with a wave of his hand.

"You're right, son," John Searles replied. "But ain't no man livin' knows them mountains well enough to figure the exact location. Only way would be to stumble onto it, accidental like."

This was disappointing to the Rio Kid for he thought he would be able to get more concrete information from Searles. However, the man did seem positive in his assertion that the Chinese were in the mountains north of here.

"Injuns at Paco say there's gold bein' mined back in the mountains," Searles went on. "They say these miners are 'monkey men.' "

"They might call 'em that because of the queues they wear," Pryor said quickly.

"That's what I figure," Searles admitted.

"If I could talk to some of those Indians," the Rio Kid said, "maybe I could get an idea where to look for Manilla."

Searles shook his head. "The Indians are plumb superstitious. They figure there's spirits hauntin' the mountains."

Then the Rio Kid described Beth Price and asked Searles if he had seen the girl.

"Come to think of it, I have," the borax miner said after a moment of thought. "I was at Paco night before last when the stage come in. I recollect seein' a gal answerin' her description. Fact is, she asked me if I knowed her pappy, Amos Price."

Interest flashed in the Kid's blue eyes. "You ever see Price?" he asked.

"Sure. He come through here a couple months ago with a freighter load," Searles answered. "Said he was haulin' mining equipment for Rey Manilla." Searles frowned. "That's the last I ever seen of him, too."

The Rio Kid scowled again. "Looks like folks just up and disappear in those mountains," he said, staring at the shimmering peaks in the late sunlight.

It was apparent that Searles had done a lot of thinking on the Chinese question. "It's bad enough we bring these fellers to this country to build a railroad," he said. "Now that it's finished, somebody's tryin' to stir up trouble between them an' us Yankees. The few Chinese I've seen recent look at me as if I'm figgerin' to eat 'em alive. I tell you, things like that has got to stop."

"An' all this trouble is just on account of the greed of two men," the Rio Kid said and slammed a fist into his open palm. "Rey Manilla an' Yankee Travers are those men!"

At mention of the Travers' name, Searles' brows lifted. "You think Yankee Travers is in with Manilla?" he asked incredulously.

"Sure looks that way," Pryor admitted and told of his encounter with the portly landowner.

"Beth Price is headin' for trouble then," Searles put in when the Kid had finished. "She was travelin' with Yankee Travers on that stage."

The Rio Kid thought of Don Barling and knew it would not do for the young ex-lieutenant to know that his fiancee was in immediate danger. He asked Searles not to mention it and the man agreed.

They ate supper that evening in the cookhouse where the Rio Kid spent his time questioning Searles about the surrounding mountainous country, and going over a set of maps covering the area. They discussed the spots where it would be most likely to find Manilla's stronghold.

The next morning, after acquiring two fresh horses for Chang Lee and Barling, the quartet was ready to ride.

"If you need any help, send word and me an' the boys'll come ridin'!" Searles offered.

"I'll remember that," the Rio Kid said. "But I reckon the four of us kin git in where a bunch of riders might be spotted."

With a lift of their hands in salute, the Rio Kid and his party rode north, skirting the edge of

Searles' Marsh. The sun was blinding and soon they cut west and had that blazing ball of fire at their backs. This was better than facing the sun glare on the dry lake.

Refreshed after a night's rest, Saber and Celestino's pinto were ready for anything, either a lope or a hard gallop . . . .

By noon they were at the foot of the Sierras. Barling was becoming more impatient as they neared Indain Wells. At least when the Rio Kid and Celestino decided to explore a canyon marked as a "possibility" on Searles' map, the ex-lieutenant put his thoughts into words.

"How about Chang Lee going with me to Indian Wells," he said. "Chances are we'll find Beth is there. I'll see her back to Los Angeles on the first stage, then join you here."

The Rio Kid did not like the proposition too well and said so, but he knew that time was drawing short. If Manilla was allowed to become too firmly entrenched it might take the military to get him out. And that was one thing Fremont wanted to avoid if possible, for the eyes of the nation would be focused on this disgraceful situation here in California.

"You get back here by sundown," he told Barling. "If you and Chang Lee ain't here, we'll know you've run into a jackpot and come an' get you."

"We will do that, Pryor," Chang Lee said gravely. "I wish you and Celestino luck."

After Barling and the Chinese youth were mere specks in the distance, the Rio Kid and Celestino rode through black lava canyons that would lead them deeper into the mountains.

"This'll be good for Barling," the Kid said after giving the matter some thought. "If he's lucky and finds Beth Price, then we'll be able to really git down to huntin' Manilla's hideout."

"I do not blame the Senor Barling," Celestino said. "With one so beautiful as the senorita!" His romantic Latin nature was coming to the fore again and there was a smile on his lips.

It was hazardous going, mile after mile through the jagged canyons, skirting boulders, pushing up through dense growths of pine. At every vantage point the Rio Kid would scan the countryside with field glasses. But they saw nothing suspicious, only an occasional deer.

This was eerie country, silent, almost untouched by the white man. At noon they rested beside a spring and watered their horses. They ate a meal of dried beef and cold biscuits which John Searles had obligingly provided.

"Thees Rey Manilla must have the hideout in the gopher hole," Celestino said with a grin as he munched the jerky.

"There's a hundred square miles of mountains where he could be holed up," the Rio Kid admitted. "It ain't goin' to be easy to find him."

They moved further into the mountains. Several times they had to leave the horses and go afoot to climb almost sheer cliffs which hemmed them in. Even though it was summer, crusts of snow still clung to shadowed recesses in the peaks above.

It was late afternoon when the Rio Kid decided they had better start back to the main road for their rendezvous with Barling and Chang Lee. Just as the Rio Kid was scanning the surrounding area before pouching his glasses, he caught a movement in the adjoining valley.

"You see something, General?" Celestino asked, noting the tension on the other's face.

Pryor lowered his glasses and handed them to Celestino. The Mexican looked where the Rio Kid indicated, then uttered a low whistle of surprise. There *was* movement over there, a group of Chinese coolies trotting down a slanting trail.

CHAPTER XIII

Mountain Stronghold

☐ Highly exhilarated at finding a clue to Manilla's stronghold, the Kid and Celestino worked their way across a hogback of granite. At last they had reached a spot among the pines where they could look straight down into a small valley, surrounded on all sides by almost sheer cliffs.

They could see log buildings down there. At the base of one cliff were two tunnels. A long line of Chinese coolies appeared, stripped to the waist, and wheeling out barrows loaded with what looked like clay from this distance. They disappeared into a long building that was evidently a smelter. Another line with empty barrows emerged from this building and re-entered the tunnel. Two heavy wagons, similar to the one Manilla had at Fort Tejon, were drawn up before the smelter.

It was a weird sight, for at this distance they could hear no sound. It seemed as if those workers down there were gnomes, scurrying around with desperate energy.

"This is it." Bob Pryor said grimly. "I reckon we've found Manilla's hangout."

Celestino had the glasses now and was searching the valley floor. Suddenly he gripped the Rio Kid's arm and nodded his head toward a huge gate of split logs. This gate blocked a narrow canyon, evidently the only entrance to the valley. Pryor took the glasses and followed the Mexican's pointing finger.

"Barling and Chang Lee," he said through his teeth.

The ex-lieutenant and the Chinese youth were being herded in on horseback to the main building by half a dozen mounted gunmen. The gate was slowly closed behind them.

Hands tied behind their backs, the two prisoners were hauled from their saddles. Chang Lee was unable to maintain his balance and fell to the ground, whereupon one of the gunmen kicked him unmercifully until he managed to struggle erect.

"The dirty swine," the Rio Kid said through his teeth.

"They 'ave run into the trap," Celestino said sadly.

The Rio Kid nodded. It was a good guess that Barling's explosive temper had gotten the better of him when inquiring for Beth Price at Indian Wells. This had probably resulted in a tangle with Manilla's gunmen.

From working with such leaders as Sheridan and Custer, Bob Pryor had acquired the ability to reach a decision and stick to it.

"You get on back to Searles' Marsh," he told Celestino abruptly. "Round up all the men you kin get and head back here."

"But what weel you do?" the Mexican asked anxiously.

"I'm goin' down there," he said, pointing at the valley.

"That ees dangerous, General," Celestino protested. "You would not have a chance."

"It's the only way," the Kid snapped. "I've got to try and rescue Chang Lee and Barling. And it's my guess that Beth Price is a prisoner down there, too."

Celestino knew that further argument was useless once the Rio Kid made up his mind. So the Mexican fell to work locating landmarks so he would know the approximate location of the narrow canyon entrance to the fortress. He would need such knowledge when he arrived with reinforcements.

Back where they had left their mounts, the Rio Kid exchanged his boots for a pair of moccasins he always carried in his saddle bags for such emergencies. Giving Saber an affectionate pat on the nose, he watched Celestino lead the dun off down the canyon.

Their plan was to leave Saber at the place where they were supposed to have met Chang Lee and Barling. Celestino would pick up the horse on this return trip and bring him into the hidden valley.

It was an hour later when the Rio Kid returned to the cliff where they had first spotted Manilla's hideout. Now he began a cautious descent. He was an experienced mountaineer and dizzy heights held no terror for him. His practiced eye picked out the rock formations that slanted down the cliff, seeking outcroppings, ledges, an occasional dwarf pine. All these would be stepping stones on that treacherous descent into the valley.

Iron nerves and perfect balance were required for a job like this. It was only the culmination of many such experiences which enabled the Kid to follow a trail that could normally only be used by a mountain goat. Any slip, a slight miscalculation and he would go plunging to his death.

As he worked his way down, he kept his eyes on the guards who were on constant patrol, rifles carried in the crooks of their arms. One guard was right in his path, standing on a rocky shelf a few feet above the valley floor.

It was a lush valley. Horses and cattle grazed at the far end. Manilla had his own beef and his own springs. He could hole up here indefinitely with no help from the outside world.

As he worked down the cliff the Rio Kid saw the constant stream of Chinese who trundled their wheelbarrow loads of clay from the mine to the smelter. Here and there a guard, carrying a bullwhip, laid the lash on the back of a faltering Oriental.

It was enough to make Bob Pryor's temper flare for he was a freedom-loving man. To see this slavery imposed upon fellow humans made his stomach turn.

Nearly an hour later he had descended halfway down the cliff. Now evening shadows were beginning to spread their purple across the west side of the valley as the sun dipped below the jagged rim of the mountains. The coming of evening brought a chill to the air.

He had carefully spotted all the guard positions and planted them in his mind. Therefore he knew where to expect trouble if and when it came.

Once he nearly fell and it was a dwarf pine growing out of a rocky wall which saved his life. His eager fingers grasped this as he pulled himself back to a shelf of rock to rest a moment. Cold sweat bathed his body, for he wondered if this sudden movement might have been seen by those below. But so far there was no indication that he had been observed.

Wiping his sweaty hands on his pants, he began to move down once more. Now he was ten feet above the guard on the rocky shelf. It was plain the guard never expected anyone to drop down from above. It was apparently his job to shoot down any Chinese who attempted a break for freedom.

Manilla could not afford to have anyone escape from here and live to tell about it.

The Rio Kid hesitated a moment, drawing his right hand gun. Then he leaped down at the big-hatted guard in the stained levis.

He felt the shock of the man's heavy shoulder against his chest, as they crashed together. The rifle was knocked aside. The powerfully-built man writhed as the Rio Kid's strong left arm encircled his neck, choking off the scream that was fighting to get past his lips.

As they fell to the rocky shelf, the Rio Kid brought his gun barrel crashing down on the man's head. The guard went limp, out cold.

Watching to see if he had been discovered, the Kid saw that his fight apparently had gone unnoticed. The routine of this mountain fortress seemed undisturbed. Quickly he ripped off the unconscious guard's shirt, tore it into strips, then bound and gagged him securely.

He was just about to work down that twenty foot trail, leading to the valley floor when he heard the *whing* of a bullet which glanced off the rock behind him. Rock splinters stung his neck. An instant later came the crack of a rifle from a great distance.

Panic swept through the Rio Kid as he tried to spot the marksman who fired again. By now the valley was in confusion. Guards appeared, rifles in hand, attempting to locate the trouble. So far they had not seen the Kid.

Another slug sang over Bob Pryor's head as he dived flat on the rocky shelf. Now he spotted the hidden marksman. There were four tall pines on the cliff above the canyon entrance. These had been stripped, bound together with cables and a lookout house built on their tops.

The Rio Kid raised to his knees, took quick aim with the captured rifle and fired. He saw the lookout fall forward to hang for a moment on the sill of his shelter. Then he described graceful arcs as he dropped spinning to the ground.

But the Rio Kid did not see any of this, for now he was backed against the cliff wall, hearing a familiar voice yelling:

"Take that man alive!"

It was Rey Manilla, who had come out of the main building and was now indicating the trapped frontiersman with a wave of his hand.

The guards rushed forward. Some of the coolies, seizing a moment for escape, attempted to race for the canyon entrance where the heavy gate was being swung into place by two gunmen. The Chinese were shot down before they had taken a dozen steps, only adding to the confusion.

The Rio Kid had dropped the rifle, and now his two sixes were blazing in his hands. One of his slugs knocked a guard into a sprawling heap. Another suddenly doubled up and rolled on the ground, clutching at a bullet-shattered leg.

The guards broke under that deadly fire. All was chaos in the valley, the yelling guards, the crack of guns and the cries of the dying Chinese.

The Rio Kid fired blindly, hoping to take as many with him as possible. He caught a glimpse of Link Dant, his narrow face contorted with hate, rushing out of the main building. At his side was Mike Jarel, with his long black hair and buckskin pants.

Manilla had gathered a choice crew of gunmen and Pryor knew it was the lure of easy money which made these men obedient, even to the point of risking their lives.

Now the Rio Kid's guns were empty. He made a grab for the rifle at his feet. As he bent over something smashed against his jaw. Lights blasted in his head and he felt himself falling.

CHAPTER XIV

"We'll Hang You!"

☐ Just for an instant, at first the Rio Kid thought he had been shot, but as he dropped he fell onto a boulder the size of a cannon ball and he knew that one of the guards had hurled it at him. Now hands seized him and he was dragged to his feet. He tried to struggle, but his muscles refused to coordinate, for he was half-dazed.

Now they were leading him across a clearing, past a long frame building filled with bunks. These were evidently the barracks where the slaves were locked in at night. He was taken past the line of Orientals who wheeled their barrows out of the mine. Although the Kid knew they were suffering the boots and whips of the guards, still their faces were immobile as they bore their fate with the stoicism of their race.

Further up a gradual incline was a small log building, heavily guarded. Through the open door the Rio Kid glimpsed powder kegs and stacks of the familiar cartridge cases used by the Union Army during the war. This was the arsenal and now he knew why the place boasted so many guards.

The guards were forcing him up a dry creek bed which ran beside the arsenal, slanting down from the main building. The water from the stream had been diverted into a wooden flume which carried it into the mine.

Near the main building a crew of Chinese worked beside a fifty-gallon tin of kerosene, filling lanterns for use in the gloomy interior of the mine. They stared at him out of expressionless almond eyes as he was shoved into the main building.

Inside he had to grab the edge of a heavy table to keep from falling. Now his eyes were accustomed to the gloomy interior. Two logs blazed in a huge stone fireplace at one end of the room, throwing a flickering glow over familiar faces, Yankee Travers and Rey Manilla.

"Welcome," Yankee Travers said, a huge, blocky shadow beside the fireplace. He was laughing so that his stomach shook.

At his side was the pint-sized Link Dant.

Manilla, a cocked silver-mounted pistol in his hand, grinned at the Kid and ordered the guards to leave.

"We have made a good catch today," he said, his dark face lighted evilly, "Barling, Chang Lee, Beth Price and now you."

"It won't do you any good," the Rio Kid snapped. "You'll never live to get away with it."

"Sure is funny," Travers said with a laugh,

"how some of these fightin' men sort of cave in when the goin' gets tough."

"I told you he was overrated," Manilla said in that peculiar sing-song voice of his. Then his smile vanished and his lips formed a cruel line across his face. "You almost ruined our plans!" he cried at the Rio Kid, rage making his voice shake. "We had the stupid Chinese in the palms of our hands. You were going to interfere!"

"The Chinese aren't stupid," the Rio Kid shot back, stalling desperately for time to give his brain a chance to clear. "You tricked them into believin' you."

"Sure we tricked 'em," Yankee Travers put in. "We promised 'em a share of the profits in the Silver Queen Mine. With the money they'd make, they could go back to China and git buried with their ancestors."

"But instead when you got 'em here, they was prisoners," Bob Pryor snapped. "When they died in their tracks, there was always new slaves to take their places."

Manilla cocked the silver-mounted pistol. "I may kill you where you stand, Pryor," he snarled. "You could have wrecked everything for us. If our system works out, we can take over other mines such as this, that ordinarily could not be worked at a profit. With slave labor, we stand to rule a Golden Empire."

"Don't kill him yet." Yankee Travers chuckled. "Let him hear the rest. Why, in this one mine alone, Pryor, there's enough silver to last twenty years."

"And we have all the property we took from these Chinese," Manilla grinned. "It all gives us power."

The Rio Kid listened to this knowing full well they never expected him to leave here so he could ever repeat any of it. And the odds were all on their side. But he had other persons to consider. Besides those imprisoned with him, there was Celestino who would be arriving with reinforcements.

"I've changed my mind," Rey Manilla said. "We should hang you. It'll impress the Chinese."

"And it'll show 'em that the Americans ain't going to help 'em a danged bit." Yankee Travers put in.

"We can make sure your death will not be easy, Captain Pryor," Manilla said with a mocking smile on his lips.

"Too bad you can't live to see the end of this," Yankee Travers told the Rio Kid. "With all the money we'll make I can buy my way right into the state capital. While the Americans and Chinese are busy fightin', I'll be governor."

"You sure got things figured out," the Rio Kid agreed.

Travers evidently mistook his words for reluctant praise. "We sure could have used an hombre like you," he said.

"I'd rather be hangin' by my heels over a slow fire than fight on your side!" the Rio Kid said with a scoffing laugh.

Link Dant, standing beside Travers, emitted a savage oath. He drew a gun so quickly that the movement could not be followed.

"Let me kill him, boss," he begged.

But Travers shook his head. "Nope, we'll let him live to see the weddin'," he ordered.

"What wedding?" the Rio Kid asked, as he stared out of the corner of his eye at the gun held rigidly in Link Dant's small, feminine hand.

"If I'm goin' to be Governor, I'll have to have the purtiest bride in California," Yankee Travers gloated. "And her name is Beth Price."

"She'd never marry you," the Kid retorted. "She'd kill herself first."

Travers and Manilla exchanged amused glances. "We was goin' to do this anyhow, but now we'll let you watch," Travers said with a grin.

Travers whispered a command to Dant, who immediately holstered his gun and tied the Rio Kid's hands behind his back with rawhide strips. Then Pryor was gagged and forced to sit in a big chair placed in a darkened corner, where he was securely roped.

He had no chance to make a break for both Manilla and Travers had drawn guns to cover him while Dant finished his task.

Dant left the room to return in a few moments leading Don Barling. The ex-officer's face was bruised, but his angry eyes still were undimmed. His shirt was in tatters and the Kid could see a criss-cross pattern of dried blood where a bullwhip had ripped the skin from his back.

"If you're going to kill me, get it over with," Barling cried, tugging at the bonds which held his arms and hands.

Dant prodded him into the light thrown out by the blazing logs in the fireplace. As Barling moved forward he caught a glimpse of the Rio Kid tied and gagged in the darkened corner of the room. Barling seemed to wilt as if some inner hope that Pryor would in some unforeseen way effect a rescue was now blasted. Seeing the famous scout tied to a chair took away the last vestige of hope.

A side door banged open as two fat breed women ushered in a young girl. It was Beth Price, her long black hair hanging in two braids down her back. She wore a neat gingham dress, but her slippers were scuffed and caked with mud.

Barling uttered an oath and tried to rush to her side, but Dant held him by the thongs which bound his arms.

"Don!" she cried, as she faced her fiance. Her face was pale and her lips trembled but there was defiance in her eyes. "What have they done to you?"

"I'll kill you for this!" Barling shouted at Travers. "Somehow I'll live to kill you with my bare hands!"

Link Dant pulled a gun at this outburst and for one tense moment the Rio Kid thought he was going to shoot down Barling in his tracks. Instead, at a signal from Travers, Dant brought the gun barrel crashing down on the ex-lieutenant's head. Barling sank to the floor with a groan.

As he fell, Beth Price tried to rush to his side, but the breed women, evidently wives of two of Manilla's gunmen, restrained her.

"I don't want to force a woman to become my wife," Travers said smoothly as he faced the girl.

"Don't worry," Beth cried. "I wouldn't marry you under any circumstances. Now I want you to turn the lieutenant and myself loose. Otherwise I'll have the law on you."

Travers and Manilla laughed. In the corner, the Rio Kid struggled against his bonds without result. Link Dant had done too good a job.

"I'll put it bluntly," Travers was saying. "You marry me an' Barling goes free. Refuse an' he dies."

The girl lifted a hand to her lips, glancing with horror-filled eyes from the towering Yankee Travers to the crumpled figure of her fiance on the floor.

"I couldn't trust you," she said weakly. "You killed my father."

"Amos Price's death was an accident," Travers snapped. "The fool wanted to help some Chinese escape and he was shot down by my guards."

"It was the same as murder," the girl flashed.

Travers' massive features did not change expression. "You've got one minute to make up your mind," he told her. "Either you marry me willingly and go at my side on my march to the Governor's chair, or Barling dies, here and now."

At a nod from Travers, Link Dant cocked his gun and stooped, to place the muzzle at the unconscious Barling's temple. Beth Price's scream was nerve-shattering as she tried to free herself from the clutches of the breed women who held her by the wrists.

"Don't kill him!" she cried. Then the fight seemed to go out of her as she turned to Travers. "How do I know you won't kill him anyway," the girl said weakly.

"You have my word," Travers answered smoothly. "You kin watch him ride out the gate at sunup."

The girl nodded her acceptance and Dant straightened up and holstered his gun. Without another word she was led out of the room and the door closed behind her.

Now Travers bellowed an order and two guards rushed in to drag Barling from the room. The Rio Kid's gag was cut and he was freed from the chair, but his wrists were still thonged behind his back. There was virulent hatred in his eyes as he glared at Travers and Manilla.

"You tricked that girl!" he cried, his mouth sore from the gag, so that his voice sounded more like a croak. "You'll never let Barling live!"

"Of course we won't," Rey Manilla purred. "Do you think we are fools?"

Yankee Travers stepped forward and slapped the Kid across the face with the flat of his huge hand.

"I've wanted to do that for a long time," he snarled.

The blow had rocked the Rio Kid to his bootheels, but he did not flinch. Now two guards seized him and hustled him from the room. He was shoved down a long flight of stairs outside the building. Now it was dark and stars shone in the velvet sky.

In the basement a heavy door of split logs was opened and he was shoved into a room, so dark he could not see a foot in front of him. Now the door was closed and the rattle of a bolt sliding into his socket told him he was locked in.

Then he heard Manilla's voice through the door as he addressed the guards.

"I want these men alive in the morning," he ordered. "Otherwise you pay with your own lives! Remeber that!"

142

CHAPTER XV

Suicide!

☐ Pausing uncertainly, with his wrists lashed behind his back, the Rio Kid stood just inside the locked door, trying to accustom his eyes to the gloom. He heard a sound behind him, then somebody was tugging at his bonds.

"Luckily I am not tied," Chang Lee whispered in his ear.

While he was being freed, Pryor told everything that had happened since their separation that morning.

"Celestino is comin' with help," the Rio Kid finished, rubbing his wrists to restore circulation.

"He can never get through the gate before we are all killed," the Chinaman said with a shake of his head. "It is a pity we have to die before our mission is complete."

Then he told of Beth Price's imprisonment. When the Kid told him how Travers had tricked her into agreeing to marry him, Chang Lee uttered a Chinese oath.

"It is hopeless to try and rescue her," he said sadly.

The Rio Kid had learned early that a spirit of

optimism usually enabled him to plan a way out of his difficulties, no matter how great the odds. As they started to revive Barling, Chang Lee told how they came to be captured.

They had arrived at Indian Wells and Barling had learned from a barkeep that a girl answering Beth Price's description had gone into the mountains with Yankee Travers. Barling lost his temper and had tried to choke further information from the man. Several of Manilla's gunmen, in town for supplies, heard the ruckus and upon investigation captured Barling and Chang Lee.

"It was unfortunate," Chang Lee concluded. "We fought, but they outnumbered us."

Now that Barling had regained consciousness and had been untied, he cursed like a madman when he learned of his fiancee's plight. The Rio Kid had to clap a hand over his mouth and force him back from the door.

"Hold on to your temper," he growled. "We got to plan a way out of here."

"My temper is always getting me into trouble," Barling said ruefully.

They compared notes then, each recalling all he could about the layout of the mountain fortress. But even this pooled information offered them no tangible plan.

"We got to do somethin'," the Rio Kid whispered grimly. " 'Cause if Celestino and the others git into that canyon, they're liable to run into a trap."

Then he suddenly got an inspiration. "Manilla told the guards out there, that if we weren't alive in the mornin', they'd be killed," he reminded Chang Lee in a whisper,

"I remember," Chang Lee replied. "But it would solve nothing to kill ourselves."

"We can make 'em think we're goin' to commit suicide," the Kid said.

Chang Lee allowed a slow smile to spread across his shadowy face. Barling slapped his knee.

"It might work," he whispered, his voice husky with emotion.

They agreed that the best time to strike would be just before dawn, so they sat huddled in the dark cell counting the hours that passed like years, while they made plans.

Then the Rio Kid went to the door where he could hear the muted voices of the two guards.

"What's killin' yourself goin' to gain?" the Rio Kid said loudly so the guards could hear.

"I will die anyway," Chang Lee replied, "I have a deadly Oriental poison. One drop is all that I need."

"Stop him, Barling!" the Kid cried.

"What's goin' on in there?" one of the guards yelled through the door.

There was a moment of silence inside the cell. Then the Rio Kid began to talk again. "I reckon you're right, Chang Lee. We all might as well do it. I don't hanker to get strung up. Here, gimme that poison bottle."

Chang Lee was groaning now. He and Barling had moved to one side of the door, the Rio Kid to the other.

Already the bolt was being withdrawn, as the guards, evidently recalling Manilla's threat, wanted to protect themselves.

Now they plunged into the cell, but before they realized the trick, an avalanche of human flesh smote them. The Rio Kid took the nearest guard, a burly hombre with a heavy brown beard. Chang Lee and Barling had the other guard. Clamping an armlock on Brownbeard, the Rio Kid threw him heavily to the stone floor. The man sighed and relaxed as his head struck the floor.

Chang Lee and Barling had their man out cold. There was no time to tie and gag the guards.

Taking their guns, the trio rushed up the heavy plank stairs which carried them to ground level.

On all sides the black bulk of the mountains rose toward the starry sky, which even now was beginning to pale.

Dawn in the mountains comes quickly and the Rio Kid knew they would have to work fast. It was their intention to capture Manilla and Travers and thus force capitulation from the guards.

Fifty yards away lanterns were glowing in the barracks as guards roused sleepy Chinese for another day's work in the mine.

Just as they were about to crash in the main

building, five men came suddenly down the stairs from the wide porch. The Rio Kid hissed a warning, but too late. In the gathering light they saw Mike Jarel and Link Dant with three guards,

Link Dant had spotted the fugitives first. Now he gave a cry of alarm in his shrill, almost womanish voice. Instantly hands dived for guns.

The Rio Kid's first slug caught Dant in the chest and sent him spinning to the ground. Bullets were slamming into the log wall at his back and guns blazed wickedly in the cool pre-dawn.

The fight was over almost as soon as it started. Now Mike Jarel lay dying and Link Dant was already dead. Two other survivors were running for cover.

"Scatter!" the Rio Kid ordered and the trio separated, after taking fresh guns and belted ammunition from the wounded.

As the Kid broke away he heard the thud of boots as other guards sped to the scene. From the main building came Yankee Travers' harsh voice, demanding to know what the trouble was.

The last Bob Pryor saw of Chang Lee was when the Chinese, like a fire-spitting demon, charged straight toward the barracks, twin guns blazing in his hands.

Barling had disappeared and the Rio Kid guessed he was going to attempt Beth Price's rescue.

It was unfortunate that Link Dant had seen them, for it cut down their chances for success.

There was almost no possibility of getting out now, but the Rio Kid was determined to wreak as much havoc as possible before they killed him.

The valley was in an uproar now. Rey Manilla was shouting orders. Guards were running blindly in the semi-darkness, trying to locate the fugitives.

Now the Rio Kid was sprinting along the far wall of the main building. Suddenly he sprawled as his feet became tangled up in a pile of metal objects. He pulled himself to his feet and saw he had stumbled over lanterns. Nearby was a fifty-gallon kerosene tin perched on the edge of the dry creek bed.

An ax was buried in a woodblock beside the building. The Rio Kid snatched this and smashed at the kerosene tin. A bullet slammed out of the darkness and *thunked* into the metal container. A thin stream of kerosene instantly sprayed out.

Now he was hacking at the tin again and this time the blade cut a gaping hole. He widened it. Shouts were drawing closer and he knew the guards had spotted him. Now the kerosene was cascading out, rushing down the slanting dry creek bed, past the arsenal.

"Cut him down!" It was Manilla's voice.

Doubling over, the Rio Kid escaped the hail of lead that poured at him. Two guards with lanterns bore down on him. Manilla's men had to be careful in the gloom, for they had been shooting each other by mistake.

This pair held their fire too long and the Rio Kid shot one and drove his ax blade into the wrist bone of the other man. The wounded guard howled with pain. The Rio Kid snatched the lantern from his hand then lashed out with his gun barrel and laid him out.

Instantly the Rio Kid hurled the lighted lantern into the stream bed, now flowing with kerosene. A flicker of flame raced down the incline past that small, heavily-guarded arsenal.

"Put out the fire!" Yankee Travers was yelling. "It's the powder house!"

Now the Rio Kid raced up the steps that led to the main building. Just before he rushed inside he saw Travers lumbering toward the arsenal, directing the fire fighting with a frantic voice. Flames were licking at the base of the log building and all available guards were rushing that way, some with blankets, others with coats to beat out the flames before they could reach the powder.

The Rio Kid lifted his gun to cover Travers, but he was suddenly screened by some of his own men who were racing up.

There was commotion at the barracks, the shrill cries of the Chinese and the blast of guns. The sun seemed to take this instant to rouse from its nightly lethargy, for the pinkish sky suddenly lightened.

As the Rio Kid cut down a guard who tried to blast him from the porch, he saw a band of Chinese charging out of the barracks, Chang Lee at their head. The Orientals, welcoming a chance to fight for their freedom or die in the attempt, were running straight for the Manilla gunmen.

Some of them carried rifles, obviously taken from captured guards, while other brandished crowbars or sticks of wood.

The Rio Kid's heart turned to lead when he saw Chang Lee go down in that struggling heap of humanity as the guards fired point blank. But there was nothing he could do now. The distance was too great. And besides there was Beth Price.

When he entered the big room where he had first been brought before Manilla and Travers, a hoarse cry brought him to an abrupt halt.

"Watch it, Pryor!" It was Barling's pain-ridden voice.

A gun flamed almost in the Kid's face and pain streaked along his ribs. He ducked aside, catching a glimpse of Rey Manilla with a smoking gun in his hand.

Manilla's teeth were bared like an animal at bay. He was going to fire again.

As the Rio Kid threw himself to the floor, he saw two things. Don Barling lay on his back a few feet away. He was badly wounded, but still breathing, Manilla had evidently shot him when the ex-lieutenant came storming into the room.

The other thing caused the Kid to hold his fire. Manilla was using Beth Price as a shield.

All this the Rio Kid saw in the instant it

took his body to hit the floor. Now he was rolling aside as another bullet smashed into the heavy flooring beside him, so that splinters tore into his cheek.

As he came to his feet, he upended the heavy table which occupied the center of the room. This would give him shelter, he reasoned. But when he glanced over the top of his barricade he saw that Manilla was gone.

"Get him!" Barling was shouting. "Never mind me! Kill Manilla and get Beth!"

CHAPTER XVI

Clean-up!

☐ Nearby the side door was open and the Rio Kid, oblivious to his own danger, rushed through. Outside, the din was increasing. Just as he reached the back porch he saw Beth Price glance back at him, terror in her eyes, Manilla was dragging her along, one arm encircling her slender waist.

Helpless to fire, for fear of hitting the girl, the Rio Kid was exposed to Manilla's gun. Now the half-caste Oriental was bringing his weapon to bear.

Suddenly the girl slumped to her knees. The movement tore herself free of Manilla's grasp and deflected his aim so that his slug crashed ten feet to the Kid's left. Manilla was trying to grab the girl, but she evaded him and began to run.

The Rio Kid fired and drove the man back. Now Manilla turned to race in full flight, as if sensing the Rio Kid would not shoot him in the back.

Suddenly the flaming powder house erupted. In the violent concussion, the Rio Kid was thrown to the ground. He saw guards tossed about like matchsticks in a high wind. Ammunition stored in the building was going off and slugs buzzed through the air.

Then the Kid was conscious of firing at the gate. He saw blue-clad soldiers and a handful of mounted cowboys charge through the opening. Celestino Mireles and Lieutenant John Michaels were leading the attack.

Picking himself up off the ground, Bob Pryor tried to find Manilla and finally saw him trying to make a break up the side of a cliff. The halfbreed, despised by all the races represented in his mixed blood, was desperate. It showed in the tense set of his dark features, in his blazing eyes.

Now the Rio Kid was racing over the ground, closing the gap between them. Manilla fired and the bullet ruffled the Rio Kid's chestnut hair. A fraction of an inch lower and the Rio Kid would have had his head split open by the slug.

Pryor's legs felt weak and his head buzzed from the concussion of that blast, but he kept going. The bullet wound in his ribs pained. Somewhere in the distance he heard Celestino shouting his name.

But the Rio Kid knew if Manilla were allowed to escape, all this bloodshed would have been for naught.

Now he was on the cliff trail at Manilla's heels. The breed suddenly turned and fired, but his aim was erratic and the slug went wide of its mark. He never got in another shot for the Rio

Kid's weapon thundered as he dropped the hammer of his gun. An incredulous look crept over Manilla's features. He took a couple of staggering steps, then toppled forward to roll over and over down the trail.

The main building looked like a hospital later that morning. Lieutenant Michaels, who knew something of first aid, was helping with the wounded. Most of the Chinese had survived and now helped to guard the remainder of Manilla's men who had escaped the bullets of vengeance.

Don Barling, his arm and head bandaged, was propped up on the floor. Beth Price was giving him a cigarette that one of the soldiers had rolled. There were tears in her eyes, but she was bravely trying to keep a grip on her nerves.

Celestino was telling the Kid how he had found John Searles gone from the borax mine on business. But there were a half dozen of his men who were willing to ride. Then Michaels had come on the scene with his troopers. Disorganized by the fight in the valley, the guards on the gate had offered little resistance.

"I thought we would never get here in time, General," the Mexican said with a grin.

Chang Lee, cut down in that first blast of lead from Manilla's gunmen, had wounds in both legs, but he like Barling would live. Now he was already making plans with two of his countrymen for restoration of the rights of the Chinese prisoners and the return of their property seized by Manilla and Travers.

All eyes in the room were on Rey Manilla who lay on the big table. Lieutenant Michaels, his young face sober, a smudge of powder on one cheek, was staring down at the wounded man.

Michaels and the Rio Kid exchanged glances. "He won't pull through," the Kid said grimly.

"That is good," Manilla said in a weak voice.

Now the Kid begged him to clear Don Barling of the murder charge which still hung over his head.

"Do one decent thing before you die," the Rio Kid said.

Manilla grinned. "It happened just as I said," he retorted feebly, his sing-song voice losing its power. "Barling shot Chang Wah—in the back."

A shudder ran through Manilla's body, he opened his mouth as if to speak again and then died.

Don Barling, the cigarette sloping from his lips, was white-faced. Beth Price clutched his hand. The troopers looked grim. It was plain the thoughts that were spinning through all their minds. Barling would have little chance to have his record cleared. Manilla, the chief witness, had refused to change his testimony by a death statement. Jarel was dead and so were the others who were with Manilla at Fort Tejon.

Just when they had given up hope, four Chinamen entered carrying Yankee Travers' huge form. The hulking man who had dreamed of political power was now a pitiful sight, blackened and burned from the powder house blast. He seemed to be only slightly injured.

Lieutenant Michaels was about to speak, but the Kid lifted a hand for silence and had the Chinese lay Travers on the table beside the body of his dead lieutenant.

When Travers saw the body at his side, he gave a shriek and tried to rise, but the Kid held him flat.

"Manilla said it was your idea for him to murder Chang Wah," Bob Pryor snapped.

"It was not," Travers whimpered. "Manilla followed Chang to Fort Tejon. He killed him, then framed the murder on Lieutenant Barling. I—I had nothing to do with that."

"But you had plenty to do with other things," the Rio Kid told him bluntly.

"It was all a mistake," Travers blubbered. "I—I—"

The Rio Kid told him to shut up. Now Michaels had stepped to his side.

"Your Mexican friend, Celestino, set me right about a lot of things," the young lieutenant told the Kid. "Manilla was making a fool out of me and I didn't know it."

"He's tricked a lot of folks," the Rio Kid said

gravely. Then he pointed at Barling and Beth Price. "You can fix things up for them now. You heard Yankee Travers."

Michaels nodded and stepped over to Barling's side. "I've made a mistake, Lieutenant," he said hunkering down beside the wounded man. "I've learned a lot since coming West. One of the things I learned is that an officer commissioned from the ranks is as good as any West Pointer—maybe better."

Barling's face lighted in spite of his painful wounds. Beth Price was on her feet now, smiling happily. She came to stand beside the Rio Kid.

"We owe it all to you, Captain Pryor," she said the smile fading from her lips. "It was all so hopeless until you came along. I—I only wish my father could have lived to see Don and me married. But I want you and your friends to come to the wedding."

The Rio Kid grinned. "I reckon me and Celestino have got other trails to ride," he told her.

Later he helped carry Chang Lee to the front porch that overlooked the battleground. In spite of the wounds in his legs, the Chinese youth wore a smile as he addressed his countrymen, who had assembled before the main building.

Using Chang Lee as interpreter, the Rio Kid told them they would receive an equal share in the silver mined here. And their property would be restored. No longer would they be prey to men like Travers and Manilla, for the whole state of California had been aroused at the treatment of the Chinese.

"And there's a great fightin' man who'll back me up in what I say," the Kid said. "General C. Fremont!"

Later, after the Kid had turned over the responsibility of the prisoners to Lieutenant Michaels, he and Celestino mounted their horses and rode out through the narrow canyon.

As they turned and looked back at the wreckage of the fortress, they thought of men like Travers and Manilla who seek to gain power through their own evil designs, only to go down in defeat at the hands of the very men they try to enslave.

"I reckon Fremont will be plumb tickled to learn how things turned out," the Rio Kid said as they rode through the canyon.

"We write heem the letter, no?" Celestino said with a grin.

"No, we'll just take a pasear over Arizona way and tell him ourselves," Pryor said.

"*Si*, and maybe we find the new adventure."

160